Georgina's Campaign

Rotham opened his mouth urgently, taking hers as he'd so desperately wanted to, plundering its depths, ripe, sweet, and his alone.

"Oh!" Georgina cried. "Yes! That's what I've been wanting, Hugh, needing. I love you."

Her urgent words brought sanity; Rotham lifted his head. They must stop—he must stop. He pushed Georgina away from him.

"No," Rotham said, answering all her unspoken queries. He forced his voice, hard and flat. "Forget this," he said. "It never happened."

Wordlessly, Georgina stared at him. Then she turned away. She had no intention of forgetting it. The Earl of Rotham couldn't kiss her like that and not love her. And if he loved her, everything was changed.

Other Regency Romances from Avon Books

Georgina's Campaign

BARBARA REEVES

AVON BOOKS ◆ NEW YORK

All the characters and events portrayed in this work are fictitious.

AVON BOOKS
A division of
The Hearst Corporation
1350 Avenue of the Americas
New York, New York 10019

First Avon Books Printing: February 1993

AVON TRADEMARK REG. U.S. PAT. OFF. AND IN OTHER COUNTRIES, MARCA REGISTRADA, HECHO EN U.S.A.

Printed in the U.S.A.

RA · 10 9 8 7 6 5 4 3 2 1

Georgina's Campaign

1

HUGH REDVERS, EARL OF ROTHAM, was sitting at his breakfast table in Mount Street when he opened a letter from Georgina Upcott that made him swear out loud.

Across the table, his breakfast guest, the honorable Fenshaw Tanner, an exquisite dressed in riding clothes and Hessians, lifted bloodshot eyes to Rotham's face and begged him have a care for his aching head.

"I say, Hugh," Fenshaw complained resentfully. "You never look like you've shot the cat after a night on the town. And in the Regiment you could drink a damned barrel of Spanish wine and never suffer the consequences. Yes, and Charlie Upcott was the same."

Rotham glanced impatiently at him and threw the letter on the table between them. "Read that cursed thing," he commanded.

Fen took in the annoyed expression on the earl's face and watched him run a long tanned hand through his reddish blond hair, disordering still further the fair locks tumbling over his forehead. "Bad news, dear boy?"

Rotham pushed himself back and sprawled in his chair, his long muscular legs spread before him. "Yes. I should say it's bad enough." He took up the letter again. "Georgina Upcott—you remember Charlie's younger sister—has brought her father and older sister up to London. Says she wants to be presented this year instead of next. Says she needs to talk to me. Orders me to appear at Upcott House tomorrow at ten, if you please. Of all the damned starts. What is it? Why are you shaking your head at me?" his lordship asked.

Fen smiled fondly at his friend. "Must be some mistake. Georgina Upcott is a schoolgirl."

"She's no schoolgirl now," Rotham grunted. He counted on his fingers. "Hardly seems possible, but the girl is seventeen years old. Has to be. It's been two years since Charlie was killed at Corunna."

Fen blinked thoughtfully. "What year is this, Hugo?"

Amused in spite of himself, Rotham grinned. The honorable Fenshaw Tanner never bothered himself with small details. "This is 1812," he said.

"Ah," Fenshaw nodded sapiently. "Spring, ain't it?"

The earl agreed. But his friend was holding up a restraining finger. "Don't tell me," he cautioned, thinking deeply. "March!" he pronounced triumphantly. "This is March, ain't it, Hugo?"

Rotham had his chair tipped back on two legs. He let it fall to the floor with a bang. "What has the month to do with it?" he demanded.

Fen spread his hands, a pleased expression on his plain, open face. "But everything, dear old boy. The month has everything to do with it. Season starts in May. Georgina wants a month or so to buy some new finery. Buried in the country like that—Sussex, ain't it?—the little thing probably looks like some ragged country miss. Can't have that." Fen was most conscious of clothes, both his own and that of other people.

"Country miss, maybe," Rotham said caustically. "Ragged, never. Georgina Upcott is extremely wealthy."

Fenshaw shook his head regretfully. "You must be mistaken again, Hugo. Charlie Upcott was at school with us, remember? He was always in the basket. In the army, too. You are thinking of someone else."

"No, I'm not," insisted Rotham. "Charlie and his sister Lizzie were born to Sir Owen Upcott and his first wife, Sarah Coates. Georgina is from a second marriage. Her mother was Amelia Gresham."

"Yes?" Fen was still in the dark.

"Georgina inherited her money from her mother, Fen. The second Lady Upcott."

"That lady dead, too?" inquired Fenshaw.

"Five years, I make it," the earl said, frowning. He sighed, remembering how Charles Upcott had talked of his family, especially Georgina, over campfires in Portugal and Spain.

And when Charlie was wounded in a rear guard action in the retreat to Corunna, he asked Rotham, who was desperately holding him up so he could breathe, to look after the girl.

"Watch over Georgie, Hugh," Charlie gasped. "Stubborn little thing, exactly like a mule. Always in some tangle or other. Good, though. She offered to buy my colors, you know. Don't," he coughed, "don't let her marry a fortune hunter." The bright red blood bubbled on his lips. "All that money. Georgie is . . . sweet girl . . . must be protected. And Papa. Poor Papa always has his head in some book he's writing. He's no help. Lizzie either . . . Lizzie . . . featherbrained."

The earl—as though to escape the painful memory of his friend's death—jumped to his feet, stalked to the dining-room window, and stared blindly at the back garden.

Scenes of that frantic dash to the sea under Moore's command flashed through Rotham's mind. He'd had to leave his comrade's body. As long as they lived, the men who made the retreat to Corunna would remember it—would dream of the bitter cold, the disorder and lack of food, the forced marches in the snow, those eighteen days of frozen hell crossing the mountains. And there was constant danger from the skirmishers and sharpshooters. Rotham himself was wounded by one of the enemy shooting from ambush, the bullet almost killing him. His men—under Captain Fenshaw Tanner's direction—had carried him to the beach and put him on one of the ships which finally came to take Moore's men home, though Sir John was left behind, dead in battle.

Invalided home, Rotham sold out. Fen left the army at

the same time. "Wouldn't enjoy the war without you and Charlie Upcott, old boy," he explained.

Standing at the window, Rotham eased his shoulder, working it gingerly. He'd spent this winter in Greece. As he explored the ancient ruins, his wound hadn't given him much trouble. Now it ached, for it was still very cold in London.

He returned to the table and threw his rangy frame into his chair. "Know something, Fen? I've come to an unpleasant conclusion. If Georgina Upcott needs bringing out, I'll have to do it. I promised Charlie. You understand I haven't been able to do anything for the Upcott girls since I got home from the Peninsula? Oh," he threw out one hand, "I wrote. Asked if there was anything they needed." He heaved a long sigh and scowled.

"Get a reply?" inquired Fenshaw.

Rotham nodded. "Lizzie sent me a note. Said they were fine and thanked me, but assured me they needed nothing. I had my secretary remind me of their birthdays and sent trumpery little nothings. Well," he ran his hand through his hair, "what can you send unmarried girls beyond books and bonbons?"

Rotham crossed his legs, resting one boot on his knee and absently pounding the shining leather with a doubled fist. "Another thing, Fen . . . While I was off digging for Greek treasures, I neglected Georgina Upcott. Should have gone down to Barham Hall, seen for myself what was going on with the Upcotts. Too late to think of that now, of course." He paused. "I shall turn my mind to staying in London and . . . How does one go about arranging a presentation?"

Fenshaw smiled. "No need to worry. Georgina's father and sister will see to all that. You needn't concern yourself, Hugh."

"Devil of a lot you know!" grated the earl. "Lizzie Upcott is a timid little mouse who hangs her head if you so much as speak to her. You'd never guess she's twenty-two years old. Saw her at my Aunt Romsey's last summer. Pretty enough, but so shy she can't hold a conversation. She kept swallowing and casting her eyes down like I was an ogre or something. And I only talked to her because my aunt asked me. That papa of hers—Sir Owen—is even worse. Oh, he can talk, but he can't remember from one minute to the next what he's doing! He's always lost in a fog, composing books in his head. Must have fourteen or fifteen fat volumes. Grant you, they're interesting. All about rock formations and such. When I get around to it, I plan to write some books myself, about the ruins I've excavated. I could write this summer if I have to stay in Town for the season, but I won't be able to go into Hampshire and explore those old Celtic fields this spring."

Fen half closed one eye and propped his chin in his hand. "Know what, dear old boy?" he asked.

"What?"

"Wife," muttered Fenshaw cryptically.

"Wife?" echoed Rotham.

His friend was nodding. "Just what you need, Hugh. A wife."

"A wife. No. Well," the earl tempered this a little, "at least not now. I'm going to marry someday. Must have an heir, you know. But I have five or ten good years before I settle down."

"Should do it this year," insisted Fenshaw.

"You're a fine one to talk, Fen. You always say you'll never marry."

"No need," Fen said simply. "Fourth son. My father, Marquess of Feldan, hale and hearty. Three older brothers to carry on the name. My grandmother left me extremely well oiled." He smiled again. "No reason for *me* to get married."

"And I tell you there's no reason for me to get married either. Not now."

But Fen disagreed. "Yes, there is. Your wife could launch Georgina Upcott off on the ton."

"Good God, Fen. I'm not going to get married simply to bring Georgina out. There must be any number of women who could help in this case."

"Who?" asked Fen.

Rotham looked blank and then snapped his fingers. "Lady Ali!" he cried.

Fenshaw blinked. "Lady Alice de Burgh? Old Viscount Wolford's daughter?"

"Yes, yes!" Rotham said. "You know Lady Ali. She does a lot of work for charities."

"Thought Ali de Burgh was married, Hugh."

"I don't mean to marry Ali, just ask her advice. Besides, would her name still be de Burgh if she'd married?" Rotham asked stringently. "I'll tell you what it is, Fen: You're still castaway from last night."

Ignoring this animadversion on his sobriety, Fen speculated, "Alice de Burgh is thirty, if she's a day."

"Yes," Rotham nodded, "about our age. And when I decide to marry, I may very well ask a woman like her. I don't want to marry some flighty miss straight from the classroom. Have her hanging all over me."

"Yes, by God!" cried Fen. "She'd never let you out of her sight, either. You couldn't go off to Greece or . . . or Turkey, or wherever it is you like to dig for things. Egypt? Never mind! You'd have to stay in Town and do things up pretty. Have to forget about Maxine Ruxton and those other high flyers of yours." He shuddered.

"Maxine is no high flyer of mine," exclaimed the earl, completely diverted. "And *what* other high flyers are you talking about?"

This Fen would not allow. "Don't try to tell me you didn't have that little ladybird—Celestine?—in a sweet love nest on Marlybone Lane last summer."

"Oh, her," shrugged the earl. "That's over and done with long ago."

Fenshaw ignored Rotham's disclaimer. "Yes, and didn't the little Ruxton tell me you were the best looking thing in or out of a uniform she ever saw? And wasn't she sitting on your lap twining herself all over you last night, running her fingers through your hair, when she said it?"

Rotham grinned. "With your little Spanish singer

clinging so tight, I'm surprised you cared to notice."

Fenshaw hastily reverted to their earlier subject. "You said you were going to ask Lady Alice for advice. Think she'll help with Georgina?"

Rotham nodded. "I'm certain of it. Heard her say once that it must be exciting to have a daughter coming out. She's well liked by the patronesses of Almack's, too. I'll call on her this afternoon and ask if she'd like to take the girls around a bit."

Rotham shoved his hair off his forehead and sighed explosively. "Dammit! I wish my grandfather were still alive. Would like to have an older man's advice."

"Colonel Milhouse."

"What?" Rotham asked.

"Colonel Milhouse," enunciated Fenshaw carefully. "Colonel Sir Percy Milhouse, our former commander. Sold out three years ago."

"Dammit it, Fen. I know who Sir Percy is."

"Ask him when you see him at Stephens Hotel. He knows Lady Alice—serves on some of those charity committees with her."

"Good idea, Fen," said Rotham, wishing that life were as simple as it appeared to be to his friend. "Care to come with me? The colonel's always pleased to see you."

"Love to, dear boy, but there's something . . . there's someone . . ."

Rotham's eyes glinted with laughter. "Your little singer! You're going to see her again."

Fen smiled sheepishly. "Ain't saying yes, ain't saying no! Can't come to eat with you and Sir Percy in any event."

Laughing, the earl went away to his study. He wrote a note to Georgina Upcott, promising to pay a call in Upper Brook Street at ten the following morning.

In Rotham's carriage, Fenshaw protested when he learned that they were not going to Tattersall's as planned.

"No time, Fen," the earl told him. "I need to see Alice right away. I'll drop you off at your place and come back to Berkeley Square."

"Obliged," Fenshaw grunted. "Think you can settle this thing by tonight? Thought I might see you at Brooks."

Rotham shrugged. "It's possible. Can't see why I shouldn't get everything squared away this afternoon. I only hope that the tiresome chit won't fall into some scrape before then."

Fenshaw opened his eyes wide. "What?" he asked. "Is the girl a troublemaker?"

"Oh, no. But Georgina is always running some rig or other. Remember Charlie telling us how she stood up to the Dowager Countess Lumley and made her let her spinster daughter, Lady Gwendolyn Ayers, marry? Seems the dowager wanted to keep her daughter sorting her embroidery silks forever. Georgina faced the countess down and when the old lady fell into one of her famous hysterical fits, told her to come off it. Said poor Lady Gwendolyn needed a life of her own. And Georgina was only fourteen at the time." Rotham shook his head. "I'd give a monkey to have seen that! And didn't Charlie say she assisted the vicar's daughter—whose grandfather is a duke—to elope with a farmer's son?"

"That was Georgina Upcott?" asked Fenshaw. "Should think you're going to have your hands full, dear old boy."

"Not me," said the earl. "Georgina means no harm. Besides, Lady Ali can keep her in line. Fancy my Aunt Romsey will help out, too, though she's getting on in years. She's one of society's greatest dragons, you know."

"Olivia, Lady Romsey?"

"Yes," the earl said.

"Not the Lady Romsey who's famous for her Tuesday evenings?"

"The same," came the confirmation.

"I never knew the lady was your aunt, Hugo! She's one of my favorites. Enjoy going to her house. Go every Tuesday evening. Think I've seen you there on occasion."

"Well, naturally I go to my own aunt's soirees," exclaimed Rotham.

"Don't follow, old fellow. Don't follow at all."

"*What* don't follow?" demanded Rotham, trying to decipher his friend's muddled reasoning.

"Don't follow that you'd go to *any* society doing. Never knew you to go before," explained Fen.

"I'm always off exploring ruins." This was a convenient excuse, and very nearly true, except that most of the time Rotham was away, he was doing work for Lord Brumley of the foreign office. This, however, he didn't mention to his friend. One did not tell Fenshaw Tanner secrets if one didn't want them spread about. Poor Fen was constitutionally incapable of keeping anything to himself. Might as well tell Fen something as Mr. Creevey; the news would spread just as quickly.

"And," the earl continued, "I stay at my country seat as much as I can when I'm in England. You know I prefer Caxton to London. As for going out in company, even if I had the inclination, which I don't, when would I find the time? In town I have meetings and lectures to attend . . . the Athenian Club, the Delitanti, the Royal Archaeological Society and on and on. That's why you never see me. Unlike you, I don't fribble away my time at Almack's."

"My point exactly, Hugh. You *never* go into society. We never see you anywhere."

The earl gave up and conceded the argument, falling silent, wondering uneasily if he shouldn't have gone to Upcott House immediately. Surely Georgina couldn't get into trouble in one day, he thought.

=== 2 ===

GEORGINA UPCOTT, MOUNTED on a black gelding and dressed in a black habit and Hauser hat, was about to leave Hyde Park when she saw an elderly lady riding sedately on a piebald mare some two hundred yards ahead of her.

Recognizing Olivia, Lady Romsey, Georgina was determined to catch her before she reached the park gate. She urged her mount into a mad gallop.

"Lady Romsey!" Georgina called, raising her voice—another solecism—causing her groom to glance uneasily at the censorious faces turned to follow his young mistress's headlong progress.

Georgina drew abreast of Lady Romsey and smiled. "How nice to see you!"

"Georgina Upcott!" cried her ladyship. "I see you're in looks, my girl. Is your sister with you?"

"Not Lizzie. She's still asleep."

"I didn't know you were coming to town," Lady Romsey said. "Lizzie didn't mention it in her last letter."

Georgina gave a little gurgle of laughter, her face lighting with amusement. "Oh, well. But Lizzie didn't know we were coming to London this spring." She pulled her horse closer to Lady Romsey's side. "I only decided to come to town three days ago," she confided.

"Ah?" Lady Romsey responded, looking Georgina over with a critical eye. "I'm pleased to see you looking so well, Georgina. Others may call Lizzie more beautiful, but I've never agreed. You girls are as different as your mothers were."

"In looks as well as character," Georgina said ruefully. Lizzie was small, a dainty blond, a vision of gold and pink, with bright yellow curls, china doll eyes, and lips like rosebuds.

"Your sister is beauty," Lady Romsey said with some asperity, "but you have brains. Besides," she added, "I always said you'd be an incomparable. And I was right. Lizzie can't hold a candle to you."

Georgina couldn't bear to hear her sister criticized and started to protest, but Lady Romsey shushed her.

"Not only that," her ladyship continued, "but you have your mother's amber eyes. Except that yours are larger and more slanted than Amelia's. And your auburn hair is a shade more golden than hers and just as long and silky. I can't believe you've changed so much in one year."

Georgina, who couldn't admire her own style of looks, blushed and murmured that Lady Romsey mustn't say such things.

"And why not?" demanded her ladyship, eyeing Georgina's almost classically perfect profile. "You're a stunner, my girl. You might as well admit it."

"Oh, no," Georgina said. "I'm sure you are only being kind." She leaned toward Lady Romsey and lowered her voice.

"Could we talk? I . . ." She hesitated and caught her lip in her teeth. "There's a favor I need—that Lizzie and I both need, Lady Romsey."

Olivia Romsey tilted her head to one side like a small inquisitive bird. "I am intrigued, Georgina. You must know I've been feeling bored lately. All this snow has left me sadly flat. After all those years in India with my dear Hait, I no longer appreciate these dank chills and wet fogs."

Her ladyship broke into a gurgle of laughter. "Come, Georgina," she urged. "I was going home. We can talk freely there and I can get you away from here. Everyone is watching. You must accustom yourself to stares and glares, Georgina, if you persist in riding pell-mell through the park."

"Oh, dear!" Georgina cried, laughing and shaking her head. "I'd forgotten. Nothing above a sensible trot. I remember now. Well, I'll be careful from now on, only I did want to speak to you before you left the park."

"We'll have some tea and a coze in my back parlor," her ladyship promised. "Or breakfast, if you haven't had yours. Have you?" she asked.

"Goodness, yes." Georgina smiled. "I'm always up at the crack of dawn. I like to be about and doing. Poor Lizzie swears that's when I do all my *scheming*. She says that while she's asleep my brain is hatching some tangle or other. That's what she and our brother Charles used to call my schemes. But this time, I've outdone myself. And I'm going to need assistance. I've brought Lizzie to town to get her a husband. I want to take her to Almack's and to routs and parties, to musicales and Venetian breakfasts—everywhere!"

"Am I to understand Lizzie doesn't know the purpose of your trip to London?" asked Lady Romsey, as they guided their mounts out the park gate and trotted up Park Lane toward Portman Square and Romsey House.

Georgina raised her dark brows. "Of course Lizzie doesn't know. She wouldn't have come if I'd told her. No, I had to say I wanted a Season in town and she must come along to support me. Even then she tried to balk. I honestly think she would have stayed at Barham Hall if I hadn't coaxed her. I even had to cry, and you know how I hate that. But you know how retiring my sister is," Georgina said.

"Yes," her ladyship smiled as they dismounted. "Don't worry, Georgina, we shall lay careful plans."

Georgina had always admired Lady Romsey's house. It was made of stone with iron detailing, four stories tall, and with a beautiful dining room designed by John Carr. Georgina was especially fascinated by the grisailles, done in pale tones of cream instead of the usual gray. She wanted to have some of the monochrome paintings done at Upcott House, depicting scenes of ancient Byzantium done in faux-relief.

They passed from the dining room into the morning room, where Georgina strode about, her quick restless energy sending her to examine the hunting prints on the walls.

"I like your riding dress," her ladyship called. "A Worth, isn't it?"

"Yes," Georgina conceded. "I really love this room, you know."

"Yes, so do I. And it's Rotham's favorite. You remember my nephew, don't you? Hugh Redvers, the Earl of Rotham?"

Approaching the table, Georgina nodded. "Yes, he was Charlie's best friend. But I haven't seen him since I was a child."

"Sit down, Georgina, and drink some tea," Lady Romsey directed. "Have you given any thought to whom you'd like to marry? After securing a husband for Lizzie, of course."

"Me?" cried Georgina. "Lady Romsey, no. I'm serious when I say *I* am not looking for a husband. I doubt I'll ever marry."

"Georgina," exclaimed her ladyship. "Bite your tongue. Never let me hear you say such a thing. What will happen to you if you don't marry? I'm glad your mother can't hear you. You know Amelia was one of my best friends. I was closer to Lizzie's mother Sarah, but I loved your mother, too, Georgina."

"Did you?" asked Georgina.

"Yes," her ladyship smiled. "I had always known Amelia— knew her in school. You realize that your mother and Lizzie's mother were my bosom bows in school, along with Jane Postlewaite. Yes, we were all friends, but Sarah and I were practically raised together. Our families were used to having both of us or neither, for when Sarah went home she took me, and when I went to Morgenmede, Sarah came too. We were closer than sisters."

Lady Romsey chuckled. "Oh, the talks we used to have under the covers. We dreaded growing up and being separated by our marriages, you see. But in our first Season, Sarah fell in love with your father, Sir Owen, and I with my own dashing captain. It seemed perfectly natural that we should put our girlhoods behind us, so eager were we to join our lives with those of our husbands'."

"Is Lizzie anything like her mother?" Georgina asked. "We have no portrait of her."

Coming back from her recollections with a start, Lady Romsey smiled and shook her head. "Heavens, no. Sarah was quick and lively and had a biting wit. The only thing Lizzie seems to have inherited from her mother is her looks. I must admit that Lizzie is even more beautiful than Sarah was."

Georgina was pleased. "Lizzie is beautiful, isn't she? Oh, Lady Romsey, will you help us?"

"Of course," Lady Romsey cried. "Oh, this is going to be great fun. I'm so glad you came to me. I'd love to be your sponsor. I'll present you at one of the drawing rooms and give you a grand ball. And we'll have musicales and rout parties."

"Thank you, Lady Romsey. Your splendid balls are famous. So many people attend. I've heard them described as the most horrifying squeezes. And to be taken about Town and included in your Tuesday evenings. Please understand, Lady Romsey, it's necessary to expose Lizzie to the beau monde. I'm absolutely certain all the eligible bachelors shall see her and fall straight away in love."

"Oh, my dear," Lady Romsey shook her head. "It's a sad reflection that marriages are made in solicitors' offices and not at Society balls. I'm afraid poor Lizzie's lack of fortune must outshine her beauty."

"Lizzie has money."

"Oh? Exactly how much and from whom?"

Georgina's chin lifted. "My mother named Lizzie and Charles in her will. When my brother died, Lizzie inherited his portion. With Papa's permission I have dowered

Lizzie. My sister says it's all a hum. But the money is hers, legally signed and sealed."

Georgina's lips tightened, remembering the scene when her sister learned they were coming up to London for the Season. Lizzie had said almost at once that she couldn't afford to buy any new clothes.

Lady Romsey's brows lifted in pleased surprise. "I hadn't realized you were rich enough to give Lizzie any money, Georgina. How much," she inquired, "were you able to give her? I don't hesitate to ask, because that fact must be tossed out to draw in the nibbles."

"Thirty thousand," said Georgina in a tight little voice.

"And added to what your mama gave her?"

"Fifty thousand," Georgina replied, drawing a deep breath. "Lizzie has fifty thousand pounds. Naturally, I'll add a jointure when she marries."

"Ah!" Lady Romsey beamed. "That's very well, Georgina! I'm delighted. A beauty, well dowered. I do not foresee difficulties with finding suitors for Lizzie."

Georgina found that Lady Romsey was eyeing her speculatively.

The older woman nodded briskly as if something had been decided. "Yes, Georgina, we'll snare Lizzie a husband. Helping young ladies is something I like to do, especially when they are daughters of my childhood friends. But I must warn you, I intend to help you, also. I can't wait to see the beau monde's reaction to you, now that you're all grown up."

Georgina looked at the strange little smile playing around her ladyship's lips. Before she could comment, Lady Romsey spoke again with barely contained laughter.

"When do you expect to see my nephew? Hugh is quite my favorite relative, you know."

Georgina relaxed. "Tomorrow at ten. I sent round a note asking him to call on Papa. I know I shouldn't have sent it, but really . . ."

"Very proper," her ladyship murmured, looking satisfied and a little smug. She chuckled and patted Georgina's cheek as the girl kissed her goodbye.

"I couldn't be more pleased, my dear child. I'm sure everything will work out perfectly. Say hello to Rotham for me, won't you? I wonder what he'll think when he sees you?" She laughed aloud and was smiling broadly when Georgina left her.

Georgina rode at a smart trot along Park Lane, pleased at the ease with which Lady Romsey had agreed to her plans.

She had to return to Upcott House for her carriage if she was going to see Sir Graham Bardolph. The widower of her late godmother, Sir Graham was her godfather as well as her financial adviser.

Georgina pulled up her horse in Green Street, letting a carriage pass the intersection. She wondered if Lizzie wasn't already suspicious of her motives in coming to town. It was only by the greatest tact that Georgina had been able to convince her sister that although she was ready to enjoy a Season, she didn't actually want a husband. She wasn't sure Lizzie believed her and she was positive Lady Romsey hadn't.

Georgina shrugged. Not many could understand her reluctance. Even if she decided to be married, who, she wondered, would she choose? In spite of what Lady Romsey said, she knew she wasn't beautiful like Lizzie. Whoever wanted to marry her would be interested only in her fortune.

She frowned. The point was, and she had to admit it, she didn't want anyone telling her how to manage her money. It was lucky that Papa never interfered in financial matters. He had never bothered with money and would have been no help even if he'd tried. He didn't understand business and was the first to admit it didn't interest him. He was content to leave everything in Georgina's hands.

Before her death, Georgina's mother Amelia, operating as *feme sole,* had handled all the financial affairs in the Upcott family. After all, the money was hers. Georgina had been trained from infancy to continue in her mother's tradition. She remembered sitting with Mama when she did her accounts, listening to lists of investments or being told of some venture Mama and her friend Sir Graham were interested in. From babyhood, Georgina had been fascinated with such transactions.

Georgina smiled. Poor Papa. As her guardian he had to sign for her, but he cheerfully did so, never questioning what she did, even when thousands of pounds were involved. Sir Owen trusted Georgina and knew that Sir Graham was keeping an eye on her.

But these pleasant arrangements would end if Georgina should marry. If only women understood what they were getting into when they became wives, Georgina thought. They were always minors under the English law. From the moment she was born, a woman was ruled by some man. First by her parent or guardian and then by her husband. A married woman's wealth belonged to her husband. A woman could gain independent status only by petitioning the courts as Georgina's mother had done. And such things must be ironed out in the marriage settlements. Few men were as agreeable as Papa.

No, Georgina decided. She would never turn her fortune over to some stranger. How could she respect a man who married for money? She'd never saddle herself with such a parasite. She didn't want a man whose only accomplishment was snaring a rich wife. In fact, she didn't want a man at all.

At Upcott House, Georgina met Lizzie on the stairs.

"Georgie!" Lizzie cried. "Dearest, you left so early. I meant to go riding with you."

"What?" Georgina laughed. "You? Since when have you enjoyed being out before noon? And on a horse?"

Lizzie smiled. Standing on the step just above Georgina, she could look directly into her sister's eyes. "I don't. But I thought I could keep you from racing Sultan about the way you do at home."

Georgina grimaced. "Too late, I'm afraid. I saw Lady Romsey and spurred to catch her."

Seeing Lizzie's horrified expression, Georgina laughed.

"Don't worry, Lizzie. I've already promised Lady Romsey that I shall become a sedate rider like all the rest. No harm done."

"Oh," Lizzie said worriedly. "I hope not. If you don't be careful, Georgina, you'll shock the beau monde and put all your prospective suitors off."

"That would be a very good thing, Lizzie. Try to remember that I am *not* throwing myself into the Marriage Mart!"

"I know what you say, dearest, but you can't be serious."

With a steely glint in her eye, Georgina grasped her sister's elbow and steered her back up the stairs. "Come talk to me a moment before I change."

They entered the sitting room of Georgina's chambers. Georgina tossed her hat on the sofa and threw herself on the rug before the fireplace. She leaned her elbow on a hassock and sprawled in the way that had driven three governesses half wild with despair.

Lizzie smiled and shook her head. "You're going to have to learn to sit on chairs, dearest, now we're in town."

Georgina looked up at her sister. "I like to sit on the floor. Don't worry. I won't do it when we make morning calls."

She smiled fondly at Lizzie and then grew quiet. "Liz, what can I say to make you believe I'm not seeking a husband?" she asked earnestly.

"Hush, dearest," Lizzie begged, firming her soft pink mouth. "This is merely one of your wayward notions. I'm sure you'll change your mind before long." She seated herself on a chair near the fire. "Besides, I'm positive that you'll *take* in this first Season, Georgina. You'll probably be married by this time next year. This could very well be the last year we spend together."

Georgina shook her head. "No, no. Like as not, I'll never marry, Lizzie. However, it won't hurt me to have a Season or two, and it will do me a great deal of good to acquire some Town bronze and make my official come-out."

"*Never* marry?" Lizzie gasped, as she finally understood her sister.

"Never," Georgina asserted flatly. "I intend to live my life in a rather unprotected way, you see. I must be free to come and go in the City and be about my business. And the sooner people see me do so, the better, I expect. And when I'm quite antiquated, I shall grow into an endearingly odd character, becoming famous as 'that rich old Miss Upcott,' whose fortune came from shipping and is said to rival Lord Trevathan's. Oh!" Georgina cried, growing enthused with her future visions. "And I shall have grand salons even more famous than Lady Romsey's Tuesday evenings and give extravagant dinners and fabulous dances in the ballroom. I'll have protégés and sponsor promising young men for Parliament. And be quite useful to *your* children, Lizzie. All of whom shall be my heirs, of course.

"And," Georgina exclaimed, coming down from her flight of fancy, "that's another reason for setting up here in London. I must be close to Sir Graham."

At Lizzie's blank look, Georgina exclaimed sharply, "Think, Lizzie."

Georgina was always a little impatient with her sister's fuzzy reasoning and reminded herself to be more tolerant.

"Be sure, Georgina," Charles once cautioned her, "that you lead Lizzie to the truth by gradual degrees. You have to measure what you tell her in small doses. Another thing—make sure she perfectly understands you, for it's the very devil to get an idea—right or wrong—out of her noggin once she grasps it."

Looking at her sister's puzzled face, Georgina modified her tone and said coaxingly, "You remember Sir Graham Bardolph, Lizzie. Well, Sir Graham is a financial wizard. I need him to teach me more about managing my fortune. I intend quadrupling it by the time I'm thirty, you know. I may even establish an office in the city."

Lizzie was appalled. "Oh, Georgina! No! You *can't* mean to go into trade. Surely Papa would have something to say about that. Polite Society will shun you. You—all of us—will be beyond the pale."

"That's nonsense," Georgina declared roundly. "Where do you think their fortunes come from—these high flyers who live in town the year-round and spend money like water? It comes from business ventures, from India, the China trade, whaling, speculations, investments—any number of things. Did you imagine it came from their country estates? Their sheep, or perhaps their rents? Unless they have thousands and thousands of acres, Lizzie, the money comes from elsewhere. Listen, do you know how much our own small estate, Barham, took in last year? No, why should you? It's my business to take care of such things. The produce from the home farm brought us two hundred pounds, including the timber I sold. I got seven hundred and fifty for wool and three hundred in rents from nine farms and eleven shops in the village. Our expenditures for the household, such as food, heat, clothing, the servants' wages, the new paddocks, replacing slates on the roof, repair on the steward's house, pensions to the old housekeeper, to grandfather's bailiff and Papa's nurse, who is ninety if she's a day, and not forgetting to add in the Reverend Mr. Crow's living—or didn't you know we paid his salary?—our expenses were twelve hundred and fifty pounds total. We made a profit of thirty pounds, Liz. Thirty pounds! So you see why I must learn to manage my money. Right now I have an income of about sixty thousand a year from the interest my capital earns in Consuls and the Funds. And I have rents from property here in London, of course. But do you have any idea what I *could* be making by investments? Not touching my principal, you understand, but using my income interest as venture capital?"

Georgina, noticing Lizzie's bewilderment, took pity and said, "No, you don't, so never mind. Only don't think there's such a stigma attached to business. Oh, retail, yes. Anyone setting up a shop would be cut dead by the haut monde. But consider this, Liz—anytime you see evidence of money, someone has made it or is making it. Only look at Lady Jersey. Her grandfather owns Child's Bank and she's his heir. But she's also a Westmorland and one of Society's greatest dragons—along with Mrs. Drummond-Burrell, the Ladies Castleraugh and Cowper, not to mention Lady Alice de Burgh, all of whom have money."

Georgina shook her finger at her dazed sister. "Remember, Lizzie. It takes money to be good ton. Or at least, one must show signs of having money. I don't worship it, don't think I do. But I'm clear on one point. It's what greases wheels in this world. I intend doing something with mine—I want to help people. So I'm going to need a lot more of it." Georgina nodded sagely. "I expect I'll end up a female Golden Ball," she finished, giving a contented little sigh.

Lizzie was more confused than ever. "But Georgina," she cried, "how are you going to know how to go on or even begin?"

"Oh," Georgina shrugged. "I have Sir Graham. And Rotham shall stand me in good stead. The earl was Charlie's best friend, after all. I've written him a note. I expect him to pay us a visit tomorrow morning at ten."

She blew her sister a kiss and went away to change out of her riding habit.

=== 3 ===

IN BERKELEY SQUARE, Hugh Rotham found old Sidney de Burgh, eleventh Viscount Wolford, on his hands and knees in his war room. His lordship was surrounded by dozens of lead soldiers, toy cannon, miniature fodder wagons, and all the other impedimenta needed to re-create a scene of battle.

"Rotham!" his lordship cried, struggling to his feet. "I'm deuced glad to see you." He shook hands and gestured at the disarray. "I'm taking down my reenactment of Talavera. You saw it, didn't you? Should hate to think you missed that."

Rotham grinned. Lord Wolford seemed to be under the impression that it was a capital treat for guests to view row upon row of toy soldiers, all advancing in frozen formation upon enemy positions.

"Oh, yes, sir," he said. "I helped you set it up last autumn."

"That was you, eh? Well, well. I'd forgot. But you're exactly the man I need. You were at Bimiera, weren't you? I'm thinking of making that my next battle. Tell me about it."

Hugh drew a deep breath, cleared his mind, and forced himself to concentrate. "You remember, sir, that Junot left a force at Lisbon and came up to reinforce Delaborde. He thought our left was weak and did a foolish thing—he attacked without reconnoitering."

"Ah, ha!" cried Lord Wolford. "But Sir Arthur's regiments—with yours amongst them—were hidden behind the heights and sprang up!"

Hugh nodded. "Yes, and we were supported admirably by the artillery. Our volleys and bayonet charges drove the French columns off."

"And your losses?"

"About eight hundred, sir. And the French lost two thousand men and twelve or thirteen guns."

Lord Wolford squinted his eyes, thinking. He shook one finger at Rotham. "I've read a great many accounts of the battle, but it's always good to have another report. Wellesley gave evidence of his extraordinary leadership there, eh?"

Not a great admirer of Sir Arthur Wellesley, Rotham felt impelled to remark, "I suppose you could say so. But there was an outcry here at home, if you'll remember. It was thought that Junot should have been forced to an unconditional surrender in the Convention of Cintra."

The viscount was shaking his head. "No, no!" he cried. "Sir Arthur signed only the armistice with Junot and not the convention. Dalrymple and Burrard did, but even they were cleared by the court of inquiry. Sir Arthur was acquitted, you know."

Rotham knew Wolford could stand no aspersions cast upon his idol. He nodded but observed a discreet silence.

After a moment, Lord Wolford asked, "And you? What happened to you after that? Where did you go?"

"Oh, Sir John Moore assumed command. That autumn we marched overland. Our regiment went with Sir John Hope through Badajoz, to Talavera and over the Escurial Pass. We were there about the time Moore reached Salamanca. We finally caught up with him just in time for the retreat to Corunna. Soult attacked us there, and Moore was killed and Baird wounded. Charlie Upcott had died near the end of that march and I caught a ball in my left shoulder in the battle. Night was coming on and Hope suspended our advance and got us on the transports for home. That's the battle you should reenact, sir."

"But we lost!"

"Yes, but Sir John Moore, with thirty thousand men, kept Portugal and Andalusia out of Napoleon's grasp. And the French had three hundred thousand troops in Spain at that time."

Lord Wolford sat shaking his head in silent admiration. Then he cried, "So many stirring battles, Rotham. I can see how well they will look re-created in their many details. But perhaps you're right. Perhaps I should do the Battle of Corunna next. However, that retreat is what I'd like to show. It was the most horrifying aspect of Moore's last command. That would make a magnificent scene. Snow! What can I use for snow?"

The earl shook his head and after trying to think of a diplomatic way to change the subject, blurted, "But that's not what I wanted to see you about, sir."

"No?" the viscount murmured absently, still engaged with the problem of snow. "Would flour do?" he asked pensively. "Sugar? Powered chalk?"

Lord Wolford's gaze sharpened on Rotham and he asked, "You didn't come to talk about my battles?"

"No," Rotham said. "It's your daughter, Lady Alice."

Lord Wolford blinked. "Alice, you say. What about Alice? Is she hurt? Where is she? Never can be very sure of the girl's whereabouts!"

Rotham said gravely, "I assume she's in the house. The butler said she was in when I asked for her."

"Why do you want her?" Lord Wolford demanded. "Has that damned girl been badgering you for money for one of her confounded charities?"

Hugh bit his lip to keep from grinning. "No, sir. I need to talk with her about something. A private matter, sir."

"Oh." His lordship waved this uninteresting piece of information aside. "Benton," he called, as the butler came in answer to the bell he had pulled. "Ask Lady Alice to come to the withdrawing room. And take Lord Rotham there. Go on." He made a shooing motion with his hands. "And Benton. After you've done that, please come help me take down my artillery."

Rotham watched Lady Alice de Burgh as she entered the blue drawing room. She was, he realized, one of those women who come into their looks rather later than usual; she dressed in half-gowns whose haute style was evident in every line. These gowns, cut in lusciously opulent materials and lacking unnecessary trimming or detail, flattered her excellent figure. He thought the colors she chose, clear reds, blues, and aquamarines, and the elegant blacks in particular, complemented her dark coloring.

The earl ran his eyes over the woman he had come to see. Lady Alice was possessed of raven hair, snapping black eyes and a pale, pearly smooth complexion. She was small and slender and carried herself well, moving with a quick, light step and with her head thrown back so the first feature one noticed was her prominent little nose.

Coming into the room in an unself-conscious way, Lady Alice smiled at Rotham, greeting him as she offered him her hand.

"How do you do, Hugh? Called to see my father, have you? How kind of you to take the time to say hello. But then, you're famous for that Rotham civility, aren't you? Won't you sit for a moment? I am working on subscription balls for the Sunday School. Have you seen Colonel Milhouse lately? I must warn you, he has told me many details of your early army career. He always speaks highly of you."

Rotham smiled. "I must thank Colonel Milhouse. I'll see him this afternoon."

"How nice," she said.

Rotham sat on the sofa next to her, searching for words to explain his dilemma.

Lady Alice smiled and said, "Well, Rotham. I see you are frowning. Surely we know one another well enough to dispense with ceremony. Is something bothering you?"

"No. That is, yes." He tugged at his cravat. "I came to ask you something. I have always felt that we were more than acquaintances, Ali. More like friends, really. And you've always been kind when I visited." He muttered, "I'm making a mull of this."

Then, seeing her sudden discomposure, the earl laughed shakily and grasped one of her hands. "You must forgive me, my dear. This is the first time I've ever asked anyone to . . ."

He was about to say it was the first time he'd ever asked anyone to help him launch a young lady onto the ton, but her stunned expression stopped him.

Lady Alice stood perfectly still, gazing at him in wonder. Her mouth formed a surprised little *O*. Her sooty black lashes fanned upward, enhancing the brilliant depths of her eyes, marking an astonishment he couldn't account for.

"You're asking me to marry you," she stated flatly.

Rotham swallowed and felt himself flush. He opened his mouth but Alice forestalled him.

"Don't," she commanded faintly, throwing up her hand. "Don't say any more. Let me think."

Rotham was thinking as well, furious at the fix he'd gotten himself into. He clenched his jaw.

After several turns about the room, Alice came to stand before him. "You've taken me by surprise, Rotham. I had given up the thought of marriage. You see, I'm being honest with you, not exactly conventional, but as you say, we are friends. Let me talk a moment, sort out my feelings. You must know that I've never felt any particular desire for a husband. I never found a man I could develop the slightest *tendre* for when I was young."

She pressed her scrap of handkerchief to her lips and continued. "I've been satisfied with my life, filling it with work for the Milhouse Trust and my social rounds. Indeed, only one thing was lacking—I always wanted children."

When Rotham would have spoken, she said quickly, "Let me finish, please, while I have the courage. Lately I've been thinking of growing old in this house after my father is gone, being left to rattle around in all these rooms. It's true that I have several nieces and nephews. I also have three godchildren still in leading strings. I can help with their education and smooth their progress in Society. But the sad truth is that no matter how you like a young person, the relationship never really goes deep. It's that *maternal* bond I yearn for. Now your proposal— so perfectly eligible—has reopened the possibility of motherhood for me. Thank you, dearest Rotham." Tears gathered in her dark eyes as she held out both hands. "My answer is a heartfelt yes!"

In a daze, Rotham took her hands in his and kissed her lightly on each cheek. He felt numb, but understood what he had to do.

"I'm delighted, my dear," he said steadily. If that was a lie, then it was told to protect her from hurt. And Rotham was sure it would be true in the future. He liked Ali de Burgh. And he was glad she wanted children.

Of one thing he was certain: Lady Alice must never learn that he had not come to propose to her. "I shall do my best to take care of you," he said, placing an arm gently about her shoulders.

Lady Alice suddenly gave way to her emotions and wept while Rotham held her. After a while she sat up, dried her eyes and blew her nose with a businesslike little honk.

"Pardon me, Hugh. I promise you I shan't dissolve into tears at the drop of a hat throughout our life together. I think the last time I really cried was when dear Hannah died."

"Sir Percy's sister? I understand that you were very close," Rotham murmured soothingly.

Inside, he was edging to panic . . . *our life together!* Ali's words echoed through his brain. Rotham would live with this woman until he died. He could see the years stretching ahead—years filled with friendship, but lacking in passion.

"Yes, dearest Hannah was Sir Percy's sister. I became good friends with her when we discovered one another working on so many of the same charities. The Orphans' Assistance Board, the Climbing Boys' Fund, the Greater London Foundling Home. Hannah was vitally interested such things, as am I. She and I spent part of nearly every day together, devoting all our energies to those causes."

Rotham was determined to keep up his end of the conversation. "I understand her grandfather made his fortune in India and was one of the first great nabobs." He wondered that he could sit here discussing such mundane details when his life had taken such a disastrous turn.

"Yes, the family is terribly new. Only about three generations old. But Hannah was a lovely, cultivated woman. The gentlest soul imaginable. She and her brother became very close to me. Have you ever been to their house in Grosvenor Square?"

Rotham shook his head and Alice rushed on.

"I thought perhaps you had. Sir Percy speaks of you so often and in the most glowing accents. I think that's one of the reasons I'm willing to marry you, Rotham. I really couldn't trust my life to anyone dear Percy disapproved of. I can't wait to tell him. He is quite my best friend, you know."

Rotham murmured something noncommittal.

Alice touched his arm. She was smiling. "I've just thought of my brother Talford. Your bloodline will satisfy even him. He has never gotten over the fact that a de Burgh came over with William." She laughed merrily. "What fustian! Do you care for such things, Hugh?"

Rotham thought she had a nice laugh. "Not inordinately," he said, answering her question. "I must admit I was vaguely aware of your line. That is naturally one of the things a man looks for when he . . . decides to ask someone to be his wife. I'm glad my children will have Wolford blood."

Pleased, Alice blushed rosily. She looked, Rotham thought, quite pretty.

"Yes!" she cried. "Our children. Oh, Hugh! I'd given up the idea of tiny fat hands clutching my hair, of dressing fragrant little bodies in soft napkins and linens. And the nursery. Does your townhouse have a wonderful nursery? I shall redecorate it, painting it in fresh shades of red and bright blue. And the windows must be covered with billowing white curtains. There must be shelves for books and games and toys and a rocking horse. And we shall have small tables and chairs and a blackboard."

Rotham felt himself drawn to Alice, in spite of himself. He was growing almost reconciled. "And you won't be very far from your father. My house is only a few streets over." His voice was indulgent. After all, he had planned to set up his nursery sooner or later. It was true, what Alice said. This was a suitable match for both of them. She wasn't so young that she would expect effusions of love morning and night, and she had a life of her own.

Alice nodded happily. "I can look in on Papa each morning. It's lucky he's so engrossed in his genealogical research and with setting up all his battles. He won't miss me. It's good for a man to have harmless little diversions like that. You're interested in architecture, aren't you?"

Rotham smiled. "Archaeology."

"I knew it was one of those," Alice said. "I'm sure we shan't interfere with one another unduly. You don't mind my society work, Hugh?"

A little daunted that she should be thinking of how marriage with him would affect her life—after all, that was usually a man's point of view—Rotham forced a hearty tone to his voice. "Not at all. I shan't worry you, my dear. And you may always count on me for a contribution to your charities."

"And you don't mind that Sir Percy and I work together so closely? I see him every day. He diverted Hannah's fortune into a trust when she died, you know. The Milhouse Trust. He named me as co-trustee."

"I'm delighted, Alice. Continue as you've been doing, please. I have no notions of interfering in any way. Which reminds me . . ."

Rotham thought the time had come to speak of what had brought him. He now embarked upon an explanation of his problem with Georgina Upcott. "I need help launching the girl onto the ton, Ali."

"Georgina Upcott?" Alice asked.

"Yes." Rotham smiled. "You remember my friend Charles Upcott, don't you? Georgina is his younger sister. She's seventeen and wants to be presented. To complicate things, she has inherited a vast amount of money from her mother and every fortune hunter in town will be snapping at her heels."

Rotham ran a hand through his hair, disrupting his carelessly brushed curls.

Alice looked at him with a dawning expression.

"I've been too abrupt in all this," he said, trying to smile. "I hope I haven't—"

"Been too practical?" Lady Alice laughed. "No, my dear Hugh. You could hardly be too practical to suit me. I applaud your good sense in solving the problem of Georgina's debut with such dispatch. But confess—if you hadn't needed my help, you might have delayed asking me to marry you yet another year."

Rotham felt his face go hot. She was coming too close to the truth. He felt honor-bound to protest.

Alice laughed. "Don't worry, Hugh. I'm only glad Georgina's situation prompted you to act now instead of waiting. And I thank you for being so honest."

Rotham swung to face her and saw tears in her eyes. "Alice, you're upset. Forgive me," he apologized. "I've been too precipitate, laid too much on you."

"No, no, Hugh," Alice protested. "None of that matters. I . . . I'll marry you and I'll help you with Georgina Upcott." She raised her large dark eyes. "I'm certain we'll have a comfortable life and grow to like one another very well, in time. I'll be a good wife, and it's my most fervent desire to become a mother."

Rotham was pleased. "I must have an heir. That certainly is more important to me than getting the Upcott girl through the Season. It's my chief reason for getting married. I hope you realize that." He was glad to be telling the truth at last.

Alice smiled. "Certainly."

Rotham braced himself. "Now then! When shall we marry?" he asked. "The Upcotts are already in town and—"

"Yes! As your betrothed I'll be able to give a ball for Georgina, and I shall furnish her with vouchers for Almack's and take her about among the *haut monde*. There's no hurry to be married, only . . ." Alice surprised Rotham by turning crimson. "I'll be thirty-one in July and . . ."

She hesitated and said in a rush, "I want to start our family right away."

When his brows flew up, she stammered, "I've shocked you. Will you think I'm terribly bold?"

Rotham laughed and stepped forward to kiss her cheek. "No. You do me great honor, my dear."

He was relieved. He had noted her tears and heightened color, her ardent expression. All were highly suspicious of just the sort of emotional entanglement that had kept him from marriage in the past. But, he thought, if Alice reserved her sentiments for motherhood, that was all right. It was natural for a woman to love her children. He expected to love them himself.

"Well," he said. "We'll be engaged, then marry . . . when? In June? July?"

Alice could only nod. Then she thought of something. "Oh, Hugh," she said, laying her hand on his sleeve. "Delay the announcement to the paper, won't you?"

At his questioning look she said, "I want to make sure Sir Percy hears it from one of us. It wouldn't do to have him reading it over his morning tea."

=== 4 ===

IN PICCADILLY, GEORGINA laughed and ran into Sir Graham Bardolph's arms. She enjoyed being hugged by someone tall enough to make her feel small. She stood on tiptoe to kiss his cheek and received a kiss in return.

Georgina stood a moment in Sir Graham's embrace, breathing in the fragrance of his tobacco mingling pleasantly with his hair pomade.

She respected Sir Graham, was in awe of his business acumen, admired the way he managed his fortune and envied his shrewdness in the art of investing capital. She smiled up at him, glad to be with him again.

In his turn, Sir Graham gazed fondly on Georgina. "Ah, Georgina," he cried, tucking her under his arm and escorting her to his library. "You've grown up this past year. Turned into quite a charming girl. All the bucks and Corinthians in London shall beat a path to Sir Owen's door."

Georgina chuckled. "Nothing could suit me better. I want them to see Lizzie. She's been out of circulation too long."

"What? Is she ready for a husband?" Sir Graham asked.

"Yes. Only she doesn't know we're here to get her one. She's painfully shy, you remember. If she had her way, she'd stay buried in the country and marry some dreary parson. But I've fooled her. Lady Romsey has promised to bring me into fashion, and I shall require Lizzie to go everywhere with me. For support, you see." Georgina laughed at the fine joke she was playing on her sister.

Sir Graham smiled and inquired, "And you, my dear? Are you ready for parson's trap?"

"Not I," Georgina declared. A grim little smile held her lips against her teeth. "I refuse to let some man gain control of my fortune."

Sir Graham's smile was understanding. "I see. Well, I approve. You are much too young to be thinking of marriage. You have some exciting years ahead of you, my dear, studying all the aspects of the financial world. You are a delightful protégée, as well as a satisfactory godchild."

He shook his finger at her. "You, my dear, have a great determination to learn. If I may say so, you remind me of myself at your age. Like your mother, you are bright and readily able to grasp the intricacies of commercial machination. And you are becoming well versed in the chance probabilities of various risk factors." He stopped because Georgina had thrown up her hand.

"Enough, Sir Graham." She shook her head and smiled at him. "You make me into a paragon. Earlier, Lady Romsey tried to say that I have grown into some kind of beauty. And now you tell me I'm about to become a financial wizard. Such flattery is amusing, but quite preposterous."

"Not flattery at all, dear child," he grunted indulgently. "In ten years you'll know all I can teach you about investments and managing money. I only wish that damned nephew of mine had even a small percent of your sagacity. Gregory Mandiford is a conceited fribble."

Sir Graham frowned, his weathered features creasing and showing his age. Then he brought his eyes back to Georgina. "As for being beautiful . . . well, Georgina, only look in the mirror. Your aunt would have been proud of you."

"Aunt Bardolph was very kind to me," Georgina said softly. "She was a wonderful godmother. I've missed her dreadfully these last three years. I know you have, too. It's too bad you never had children."

An expression of sadness touched Sir Graham's face, and he looked down at his mottled hands. "Yes," he said heavily. "Hortense and I wanted children." Resolutely he straightened. "But I have you, Georgina. You must know I'd do anything in my power to help you."

Georgina was touched at this evidence of his love. Determined to lighten his mood, she said, "Tell me about the *Trident*."

This question about one of Sir Graham's Indiamen launched him into an accounting, as she'd hoped it would, of his latest adventure in trade.

So fascinated did Georgina become that it was half an hour before she could tear herself away.

"Oh," she cried with a glance at the clock. "Look at the time! I must drive by Bond Street before going home. But before I leave, I want to invite you to dinner tomorrow night. I don't know who else shall be there, but no one you dislike, Sir Graham."

"I'd never dislike anyone I found in Upper Brook Street, my dearest Georgina," Sir Graham assured her gallantly. "Which reminds me. I plan to start introducing you to a circle of my business friends. Shall I take you into the city for a nice meal next week?"

Georgina's eyes sparkled. "I'd like that."

"We'll discuss it tomorrow evening," Sir Graham smiled, as they walked arm in arm back to the entry hall.

"Ah, Georgina," he exclaimed. "You're going to go far. Only remember what I've said, my child. In dealing with your fellowmen, hold honor high and your dividends shall be great."

Georgina hugged her godfather's arm. Sir Graham had the habit of falling into a financial metaphor whenever he counseled her, whether by letter or in person. "The Golden Rule," he declaimed. "That's the ticket. It always pays off."

In the lobby of Stephens Hotel, Rotham spotted Colonel Sir Percy Milhouse and threw up his arm to attract his attention. The area was strewn with rucksacks and various packs of baggage belonging to the military men who congregated at the hotel.

The clientele at Stephen's was almost exclusively male. It was a pleasant place, Rotham thought, where a man could always find good company and good food.

Gazing about him, he thought the lobby was even more crowded than usual. Men talked, laughed, and wandered about, visiting in an agreeable maze of confusion.

Rotham shook off his abstraction and observed his old commander closely as they shook hands. It had been some time since they'd last met.

Sir Percy's tall physique, with its usual erect bearing, was trim as ever. His powerful shoulders, revealed in the subtle perfection of a coat which could only have been tailored by Weston, were carried well back. His broad chest tapered to a lean waist. The fashion of the day—the lines of the trouser legs held taut by a bootstrap, molding the thighs—was admirably suited to the colonel's figure. His thick black hair, only lightly frosted with gray, curled into military sideburns along his cheeks, and his healthy complexion was ruddy.

"My boy, I'm happy to see you," Sir Percy said, his grin revealing strong white teeth.

As Rotham responded, he made an effort to force his fateful interview with Ali de Burgh from his mind.

Meeting Sir Percy's pale blue eyes, he remembered how they could freeze a junior officer caught lacking in some respect. The colonel was smiling now, the laugh lines deepening above his tanned cheeks.

Hugh suddenly wondered why Sir Percy had never taken a wife. The colonel must be going on forty-seven or forty-eight, he figured. It was general knowledge that his father had gone to India, made a fortune, and died there. And although Sir Percy had no family, as such, Society had been known to overlook the lack of ancestors in a man as rich as Colonel Milhouse.

"Heard you were in Greece," Sir Percy said. "Or was that a story put out by the foreign office?" The colonel was aware that Rotham was frequently out of England doing undercover work.

"No, I was in the Aegean," Rotham said and hesitated. "I need to talk to you about one or two matters after we eat, sir."

Sir Percy nodded and began to talk pleasantly about various things he was doing, mentioning Lady Alice de Burgh almost at once.

"I understand that you and Lady Alice are involved in administering your sister's trust."

"Yes. The Milhouse Trust. Lady Alice and I are joint trustees."

The colonel seemed to hesitate and then said, "Ali de Burgh is a wonderful woman. She's kind and sensible and quite astute. I'm lucky to have her for a friend. It's my great honor to work with her, to escort her about, to drive her in the park or ride with her. She's a delightful companion. I believe she misses my sister even more than I do. We have that as a common bond, you know."

The colonel then turned the talk to the war news.

The meal progressed smoothly, and when it was over Rotham signaled to the waiter to clear the table and bring a fresh pot of tea.

"Do you remember Charles Upcott, Colonel?" Rotham leaned forward to light Sir Percy's thin Spanish cigarillo before lighting his own.

Waving away the smoke curling round their heads, Sir Percy nodded. "Upcott? Yes. He fell in the retreat to Corunna. You were wounded in the battle, weren't you?"

"That's right, sir. Charles asked me to care for his sisters as he was dying. Especially the younger, Georgina. All quite unofficial, you understand."

"Yes, go on."

"The Upcotts are in town; Georgina wants to be presented to Society."

Sir Percy's thick brows flew upward and he gave a mirthless chuckle. "Well," he said, "I must confess I'm at a stand. I have no more idea than a Spanish flea how to fire a girl off on the ton."

He leaned back in his chair and shook his head in a puzzled way. After a little he said, "It's too bad you aren't married, my boy. Your wife could do it."

Redver's jaw set. "Yes, sir. That's the other thing. Of course it's strictly confidential. The truth is, I went to Berkeley Square earlier today to ask Ali de Burgh's advice about Georgina. She misundersood something I said and thought I was proposing. I . . . I do like Ali, sir. I agree when you say she's a wonderful woman. I wouldn't hurt her feelings for anything in the world. So I made a recovery and pretended I had meant to propose all along. It doesn't really matter. I'd just as soon have Ali for a wife as anyone, I guess. She will make a wonderful mother for my children. We . . . discussed setting up our nursery. I'm happy about that. Only I didn't expect it to happen so quickly." Rotham tried to smile. "I suppose you must wish me happy, sir."

Sir Percy's face looked so wooden and he was silent so long that Rotham looked at him sharply.

When the colonel spoke, he seemed to be forcing his words. "Lady Alice?" he said at last. "You're going to marry Lady Alice de Burgh? I hadn't realized you were so well acquainted with her."

"I've known Ali de Burgh all my life and am pretty well used to her. Our fortunes match and her family is even older than mine. But it still seems strange that we're to be married."

"No, it doesn't." Sir Percy's voice sounded harsh, but it was rock steady. "Most natural thing in the world. Furthermore, it will be a good marriage. I wish you both well." He stood abruptly and offered his hand. "I really must be off. I'm going out of town tonight, and . . ."

Bewildered at his commander's sudden departure, the Earl of Rotham watched Colonel Milhouse rush away, saw him almost stumble as he wove his way amongst the linen-covered tables.

In Bond Street, Georgina Upcott spied Lord Collingswood Saltre on the toddle and leaned perilously from the window of her carriage. "Lord Saltre!" she called. "Colly!"

Colly stopped dead in his tracks as the Upcott carriage was brought to the curb with a flourish. A footman leapt to the pavement, threw open the door, and let down the steps.

"Colly Saltre!" Georgina cried again, alighting from the vehicle and moving forward with her hand extended. "You're exactly the man I want! I need your help!"

It had been three years since Georgina had seen Lord Collingsworth Salter, her sister's cousin. She smiled and exclaimed at his being in town.

"Will you help me?" she begged.

Appealed to in this fashion, Colly Saltre visibly expanded. "Well, well," he cried. "If it isn't little Georgie Upcott. I thought you were stuck in Sussex."

He bowed over Georgina's hand, his corset creaking only slightly. "Now what has you in a bother? Not in another of your infamous tangles, are you?"

Colly straightened to his full height and beamed down at Georgina. "Don't worry, my dear. Only tell me what it is, and I'll fix it up tight as a tick!"

"No, nothing is wrong," she assured him, gazing at Colly in awe. Georgina had forgotten how big he was. He must stand at least four inches over six feet, she decided.

"Elizabeth is well, I take it?" he asked.

Colly's girth seemed to be increasing each time Georgina saw him. He must get his bulk from the Saltres, she thought. Lizzie was related to him on his mother's side, the Coates side, and both she and the late Mrs. Saltre were tiny women.

"Yes," she said, "Lizzie is in the best of health."

"I'm glad," smiled Colly.

"We can't talk in the street. Perhaps you would like to come to Upcott House for a late luncheon?"

Colly beamed. "That would be grand. I accept. I shall be delighted to see Elizabeth."

"Lizzie will be so pleased to learn you're in London,

Colly. Only last week she was reading one of your letters and wondering when we'd see you again. Knowing you are a part of her family means a lot to my sister."

"Yes, yes," he agreed, sighing heavily. "I quite understand how she feels. Elizabeth and I are the only ones left with any Coates blood. My mother was a Coates, you know. She was Elizabeth's grandmother's cousin."

"I remember," murmured Georgina. In the past, she had listened while Colly and Lizzie discussed their convoluted family history for hours on end.

"Shall we be on our way?" she suggested. "There's plenty of room in the carriage. I've just sent my maid into one of the stores to make some purchases. Here she comes now.

"John," she said to a young footman in the Upcott livery, "take the boxes from Gilly. Oh, and you can come back later if there are too many. Gilly, sit on my side, so Lord Saltre has plenty of room."

She stepped into the carriage. "I'm ready to go," she said and laughed. "And I must admit that I've been thinking of food for the last hour."

In no time at all, Colly was installed in the Upcott carriage. Georgina immediately began telling him of her scheme to get Lizzie riveted.

"It's a design of mine," she said, "to—" Georgina stopped when his lordship held up his hand.

"I should say, rather, a *campaign*, my dear." Colly smiled.

"A campaign?" inquired Georgina.

Colly's expression was complacent. "Yes. I rather pride myself on my usage of the King's English. You will remember that I have something of a literary turn. I'm forever dashing off poems and essays, especially when the Northumberland winters keep me by the fire days on end. My dearest mama had my writings bound in three volumes of blue cordovan, stamped in gold, you understand. Mama gave them a place of special prominence in the library at Wetherfield. They're there now, ranged alongside my collection of books on great battles from ancient to modern times. Yes, Georgina. You most definitely are engaged upon a campaign."

Georgina remembered that Colly was enamored of the military. When Charlie, Hugh Redvers, and Fenshaw Tanner went into the army, his lordship had written Lizzie that he felt a strong inclination to follow.

But, Colly wrote the Upcotts, his mama had demurred. She reminded him that his father was dead and he was the only surviving Saltre. This, Colly said, was beside the point insofar as he was concerned; he had assured Mama that he had no intention of getting himself killed.

"However," he wrote, "Mama has ever been astute. She has kindly pointed out that I do not actually *enjoy* riding. In addition, she reminds me that I like to sleep in my own bed. And she has capped her argument," Colly confided, "by suggesting that I wouldn't relish scrawny chickens or rabbits thrown into a camp cookpot and scoffed down between forced marches. I believe that Mama has saved me a deal of discomfort. I shall henceforth content myself with reading of the war."

"I wish I might see your military books," Georgina said. "I understand you have a comprehensive collection."

"Yes," Colly agreed, and offered to prepare for her a list of all the books he had ordered on the subject.

"When I decided not to go in the army," he said, "I commenced an ongoing correspondence with several military experts, including Lord Wolford, two retired generals, Cousin Charlie, and Hugh Redvers. Dear Mama, before her untimely demise last summer, was keenly interested when I explained all the strategy and the tactics used in various Peninsular campaigns."

"Ah," was all Georgina could think to say. Her carriage rumbled over the cobbles taking them closer and closer to Upcott House where she could turn Colly over to Lizzie.

"I'm pleased," Colly said, after apparently having thought it over, "that I find myself in a position to offer you some advice, Georgina."

He drew his breath heavily through his nose in a way

Georgina had forgotten and said, "If I am any judge, and I flatter myself that I am, this endeavor to secure Lizzie a husband shall require extensive planning, a great deal of machination, even conspiracy."

Georgina held her breath while Colly paused and seemed to be cogitating.

"Well," he asked, "what are you doing now except recruiting me for your staff?"

Georgina blinked and Colly smiled in a satisfied way. "Yes, Georgina, the more I reflect, the more certain I am that this whole affair of yours could be thought of in the light of a military campaign." He seemed pleased with Georgina's reaction.

"Military campaign?" she repeated in a fascinated tone. Her smile deepened. "Yes, I suppose one could call it that."

She didn't care what Colly called her plan so long as he remembered to keep it secret. She began to stress all the reasons Lizzie mustn't know, but his lordship cut her short.

"Yes, yes, I understand perfectly, Georgina. We operate under sealed orders."

= 5 =

AFTER FIRST DROPPING by his own house to extract something from the vault in his library, Rotham made his way on foot to Wolford House, Berkeley Square.

He needed time to think. So much had happened; he couldn't get used to it all. And why had Sir Percy behaved so strangely? He could have no objection to Lady Alice. In fact, his conversation during their meal had centered on her. It was almost as if the colonel were in love with Lady Alice, he talked about her so much. Only—if Sir Percy wanted Ali de Burgh, why hadn't he asked for her years ago?

Rotham ascended the steps of the de Burgh mansion. Perhaps it was his imagination, but the news of his betrothal seemed to have shaken the colonel badly. Rotham couldn't understand it. He shrugged and pulled the bell.

When the door was thrown open, he asked to be taken to Lord Wolford's battle room. He found the viscount busily stowing miniature soldiers in a large box.

As Rotham was shown in, he heard his lordship address the butler. "Benton, make up a list. I want to start on Corunna in the morning and—"

Lord Wolford stopped in midsentence and stared at the earl. "Rotham!" he cried. "You're back. Came to help me, did you? Too late. Benton and I have just disassembled the cantonments and now . . ."

Feeling suddenly nervous, Rotham interrupted. "May I speak with you, sir? Alone? It's about Lady Alice."

"Didn't you see her earlier?" demanded the old man.

"Ah . . . yes sir. I did." Rotham shot a glance at the butler, who remained impassive.

"Never mind Benton, m'boy. I don't have secrets from him."

With a rush, Rotham said, "I've asked Lady Alice to marry me, sir."

The viscount stared at Rotham a moment. "Is that all? Nothing to do with me, y'know. Girl's old enough to make up her own mind. Should've thought she'd given up thinking of bridals long ago. Well," he grunted, waving his hand, "for what it's worth, you have my permission. I suppose her answer was in the affirmative?"

Rotham swallowed. "Yes. And thank you, sir. If I may see her again. . . ."

"Mustn't stand on ceremony, m'boy. Member of the family now. Come and go as you please." Lord Wolford had already turned to his demolished battle.

In his betrothed's sitting room, Rotham produced a large, old-fashioned ring which had belonged to his grandmother.

"I neglected to mention a ring, Alice. Thought I'd pop around and give you this. It was all I could find in the vault at home." He slipped the ring on her finger. "If you don't like it, you must tell me."

"It's all right," Alice said. "It doesn't really matter what the ring looks like, does it?"

This attitude did not strike Rotham as unromantic. It happened to fall exactly in with his notion of how a woman should view an engagement ring.

"Not too big?" he asked.

"Only a little." Alice smiled. "I'll have it taken up at Rundell and Bridge. There's plenty of time. I shan't wear it until we announce the betrothal."

Rotham kissed his intended's hand and left, realizing at last that he was indeed engaged to be married. He was growing accustomed. At least the problem of Georgina Upcott was settled.

When Georgina's carriage arrived at Upcott House, she was surprised to discover a stagecoach in the street, large and handsomely appointed, of the kind one encounters carrying passengers cross-country and piled high with luggage.

So busy was she in eyeing this enormous contraption, pulled as it was by four magnificent Clydesdales, perfectly matched and with flowing hocks, that she had no time to notice the driver with his furled whip nor the postilion astride one of the leaders.

As she, along with Colly, stood gaping, the door opened and a tall slender young man languidly descended to the pavement. It was a moment before Georgina recognized Lazlo "Lazy" Symonds, dressed in a driving coat with fifteen capes and wearing one of the new low-crowned beavers.

"Hullo, Georgina," drawled Lazlo. "How do you like our stagecoach?"

If the information that Lazy Symonds was the owner of the equipage she was seeing wasn't enough to floor Georgina, hearing herself hailed familiarly from the driver's box was.

"Georgina!" cried the person seated there. "Look at me!" This was Mr. Tempest Story Granville, "Tessie" for short. He wore a cocked hat and frieze coat, with a muffler trailing round his neck.

Georgina, never slow, shouted with laughter and spun for a look at the postilion. Sure enough, it was her cousin, Dexter Philbin, Viscount Chute, dressed in silks and tall boots. He wore only one spur.

Lord Chute, at nineteen and a quarter, was the eldest of the Trio composed of Sir Lazlo, Tessie, and himself. Georgina had known them all her life, for their homes were in the Sussex countryside, close by Barham Hall.

Georgina stepped back as her cousin Dexter slid from the back of the left leader. A girl couldn't have three better friends, she thought.

Dexter, Lazlo, and Tessie had gone to Eton together

and were now in their second year at Oxford. The "Triumvirate" Charlie had dubbed them; the "Terrible Trio" was what they were called at home by the neighbors and at Oxford by the beleagured dons.

Georgina smiled. They were always ripe for any lark and, in times past had dragged her along.

"Good old Georgie" they'd called her, or "Stringbean," because she was so skinny. Later, after she'd been to school and gotten long skirts, they had called her "Mrs. Georgie Bean," saying she needed a more grownup title.

Now, standing before their wonderful stagecoach, Georgina realized how much she had missed her old friends. She spread her arms wide.

"What are you three up to?" she demanded with delight. "Don't tell me you've *bought* this thing! Are you down from Oxford?" Her eyes narrowed. "Have you been rusticated again?"

Her friends exchanged slanted looks and assumed innocent expressions.

"Someone put a pig in Chewy Peckham's room," volunteered Tessie, grinning.

"The dons thought it was us," Dexter exclaimed indignantly.

Lazy maintained a dignified silence, crossing his arms and leaning nonchalantly on the door of the coach.

"You didn't?" Georgina demanded.

"No, but it was a good notion. Or don't you think so?" inquired Dexter.

Georgina pursed her lips and frowned. "Lacked imagination, is what I think."

The Trio nodded solemnly and Tessie said, "It's a shame you're a girl, Georgina. We was discussing it just the other night. With you at Oxford, there wouldn't be a dull moment."

They all, including Georgina, nodded gloomily.

Then Georgina brightened. "So you are rusticated!" she cried. "And you've got yourselves a stagecoach?"

"Yes!" came the answer in chorus.

"Well, come inside for lunch," Georgina grinned. "Unless you're not hungry."

But they were; they had known for ages they could depend on the Upcott cook for a handout.

"Thank you," Lazy said.

"Was hoping you'd ask," mumbled Tessie.

"I'm very hungry," Dexter admitted.

Georgina, Lazlo, and Tessie burst into guffaws because old Dex was always hungry—or thought he was. The boys referred to him as "the Gut."

Her eyes dancing, Georgina said, "Let's go inside and see what Mrs. Mucklesby has prepared."

Georgina started up the steps but paused at the top. "You know Colly Saltre," she said, reminding the Trio of their manners.

"Oh, Hutchins," she called to the butler as she stepped inside. "I've brought some people home for lunch."

Georgina had the meal served in the walled conservatory. There was ham and roast beef, breads and cheeses, various sauces for spreads, and the remains of last night's mutton pie. This was removed with fruit and spice cakes served with wine.

Her father came from his library and nibbled a few bites. Sir Owen greeted everyone heartily but soon lapsed into his writer's reverie. He smiled absently when the conversation did not interest him.

Georgina placed Elizabeth next to Colly. Lizzie's face held a soft glow at her pleasure in her cousin's company.

The Trio, after explaining how they came to buy a stagecoach, said they'd come with an offer to carry Georgina and Lizzie, and Lord Saltre, of course, to the park that afternoon.

Georgina clapped her hands. "Do you know," she exclaimed, "I don't think I've ever ridden in a stagecoach!" She turned to her sister. "Will you go, Lizzie?"

Lizzie smiled and said she'd like it very much, but only if Colly wanted to.

"Oh, I'm sure he does," cried Georgina.

When Lord Salter had accepted, Lazy turned to Sir Owen. "And you, sir? Plenty of room, y'know."

"Ah, no," Sir Owen said, smiling gently. "I must . . . I'm busy with . . ."

"We understand, sir," Tessie told him. "Some other time."

As they rose from the table, Georgina said, "It's decided then? You'll come for us at five?"

The Trio nodded.

"Now," Colly said. "I should like some moments with Elizabeth. I'm sure she has been waiting all through our repast to hear about my mother's funeral."

Georgina, avoiding the Trio's eyes, said as gravely as she could that she was certain this was true. Swallowing her laughter, she invited the boys up to her study.

This sitting room, three stories up, was long and low pitched with a beamed ceiling and a fireplace on a wall of shelves. Heavy leather chairs and a massive sofa were grouped about the Adams fireplace. The alcove held a Queen Anne desk piled with ledgers and journals. Near the window, Georgina had placed a game table. This was surrounded by conversation chairs in the style of Louis XV, with padded shelves atop the backrests so those watching games in progress could do so without disturbing the players.

Georgina and the Trio, after running pell-mell up the stairs, arrived in a rush to slam the door and collapse laughing.

"What a *clunch* your cousin is, Georgina," gasped Tessie. He threw himself into a chair, wiped his eyes, and grinned. "Whoever wants to hear about a funeral?"

"Oh, exactly!" Georgina held her middle and groaned. Her stomach ached from laughter. She shook her head. "However, I expect Lizzie did. She, by the way, is Colly's cousin, not I. Except for Lizzie, Colly has no other family. No, there is an old grand-uncle on his father's side. Unless he's dead."

"In which case," drawled Lazlo, "Colly can tell Lizzie about his funeral."

47

This set them howling again—all except Dexter, who remained silent. He smiled throughout, playing cat's cradle with a string from his pocket.

Suddenly he spoke. "It's like us, Georgina."

His companions were accustomed to Dexter's habit of making oblique statements out of context and sometimes days later. A little digging usually revealed he had been thinking something over and in his measured way was ready to comment.

"How's that, dear?" Georgina asked.

"Cousins. Your mother was my father's cousin. And Tessie is my first cousin."

"That's right."

But Dexter was frowning. "So what does that make you and Tessie?"

"Tessie and I aren't related, Dex."

Dexter shook his head. "No, you must be."

Georgina patted his knee. "No. Don't you see? I'm related on your father's side and Tessie is related on your mother's."

Dexter said slowly, "Don't seem possible. You're both cousins to me but not to each other?"

"No, we're not," was all Georgina could think to say.

"Too complicated for me," Dexter said after a while. Rising from his chair, he restored his string to his pocket. "I'm going to the kitchen and talk to Mrs. Mucklesby. Ask when she's making Eccles' cakes. I'm partial to Mrs. Mucklesby's Eccles' cakes, y'know. I'm deuced glad you brought her to town, Georgie."

Georgina shook her head as Dex closed the door. "How," she inquired, "does he pass the time at university? Does he ever learn anything?"

"Lord, yes." Tessie spoke from the bookwall. He stood with a volume in his hand, having, in his restless way, removed it from a shelf to flip the pages. "He told me Chaucer might have been a great writer if only he'd taken the trouble to learn to spell proper English!"

Lazy Symonds had assumed a prone position on the

couch, casting his hat over his face. Voice muffled, he said, "Never misses a class. Sits there playing with his string. Goes to church, too."

"Why?" Georgina asked baldly.

"Says it's peaceful there."

"Spends most evenings playing that piano in his room," revealed Tessie.

"Oh, well. So long as he's happy," Georgina said.

Tessie shrugged. "He is, and he loves our stagecoach."

Georgina struck herself on the forehead with the heel of her hand. "That's why I brought you up here! When can I drive the—what did you call it—Silver Cloud?"

"Told you she'd want to," said Tessie to his friend.

"You must have known I would, the minute I saw it," Georgina exclaimed. "Where do you keep it?"

"Have a house in Hampstead," explained Lazlo. "Belongs to my guardian. Said we could live there and be out of the way. Advanced me my share to buy the Cloud."

Georgina knew Lazlo's father had left his inheritance tied up until he was thirty.

"What did your guardian say when you were rusticated?" she asked.

"Oh, Rotham is a great gun. He laughed and said we could rest up for a fresh assault this fall."

"You're Rotham's ward?" Georgina was surprised.

"Yes. Seems as free and easy as your papa. Never noticed Sir Owen kicking up a fuss about funds."

"Papa is in nominal charge of my money until I'm twenty-one or until I marry, but I actually manage it. With Sir Graham Bardolph's help."

Lazlo sat up and swung his feet to the floor. "Good thing you understand stuff like that. Rotham manages mine."

"Yes, I'm quite knacky when it comes to finance."

Tessie, whose father was hale and hearty but close fisted, grinned and said money was no problem if you didn't have any.

"You get an allowance every quarter," protested Georgina.

"Yes," Lazlo grunted, "and he spends it the first two weeks."

"Do you, Tessie?"

"Devil-a-bit," Tessie replied, sticking his hand in his pocket. He withdrew some crumpled notes and several coins. Counting it, he said, "I've still got two pounds, six."

Georgina knotted her brow. "But haven't you just had quarter-day?"

"Yes. Spent it on the Silver Cloud. And coats and whips don't come cheap, y'know!"

"How does Dex get along?" Georgina asked. It was her cousin who must feel the pinch; Dexter's father, the Duke of Bede, was notoriously poor.

Lazlo smiled. "Dex throws his allowance in a drawer. Would give it all away if we let him." Lazlo got to his feet and fitted his hat over his black curls.

"Come, Tessie. Let's collect Dex from the kitchen and be on our way. Georgie, you hatch a plan for sneaking out to Hampstead next week. You can drive the Silver Cloud all over the heath."

"Yes, I will!" Georgina cried. Then she thought of something. "Before you go, I want to tell you that I brought Lizzie to town to get her a husband. I had to say I was ready for a Season or she wouldn't come."

"*You?*" hooted Tessie. "You're never going to play twinkle-toes at Almack's! That's a sight I'd like to see."

Georgina raised her brows. "You will. I expect you to dance attendance on me every step of the way. My dependence is on you three and Rotham."

"Oh, no," Tessie cried, horrified. "I ain't squiring you about, Georgina."

"Listen, Tessie," Georgina said fiercely. "Remember how I saved you from Mallon Pond?"

"Yes. And who pushed me in?" was the acerbic rejoinder. "Ask for something else, Georgina. Ton parties are too much."

"No, they ain't," interjected Lazlo. "We'll stand true,

Georgie." He shot a minatory glance at Tessie, who subsided, fuming.

"We'll pick you and Lizzie and Company up here at five for the drive in the park," Lazlo said. He pushed the scowling Tessie before him and departed Georgina's study.

=== 6 ===

ROTHAM WAS UNPREPARED for his meeting with Georgina. At their last encounter, she was about ten or eleven, thin, awkward and nursing a misshapen jaw, waiting to be taken to a tooth drawer.

He walked to the window and pulled the curtains aside. So much had happened since then, he thought. Charles Upcott died in his arms in a mountain pass in Spain. Now Georgina was old enough to be presented, and he was an engaged man.

A voice hailed him from the arched doorway and he turned to behold Georgina.

At the sight of her, Rotham swallowed. There was a finely drawn thoroughbred quality about her; the long lines of her body were clean and pure and she was extremely slender. He hadn't imagined her so beautiful.

When Georgina offered her hand, he took it and looked into her deep amber eyes. They were searching his candidly.

"You look so much older than I expected," he blurted.

Georgina whooped with laughter. "Hugh! No wonder you're not married. You don't meet a woman and immediately tell her she looks old."

He grinned and tightened his grip on her hand. She hadn't changed after all; she was still the irrepressible Georgina that Charles had spoken of.

Rotham relaxed a little. He had come prepared to act the part of a brother. It was obvious she expected the same; her greeting was that of a sister.

"Sorry," he said. "Not older. Different." His voice was raspy and he cleared his throat.

Georgina lifted winged brows. "But how am I different, Hugh?"

Rotham watched her soft mouth curve into a gamine smile. Her long slanted eyes were dancing, teasing him.

"Taller," he managed. This creature, he thought. Was she still the child Charles described? Able to fly into a fury? Or had the years tamed her into a more conventional pattern of womanhood?

Rotham found himself hoping she hadn't changed too much. He had liked the child Charlie described: a delightful hoyden ready for a romp with the Trio, with a fiercely loyal turn of nature, precociously wise, loving and kind.

He must guard her. He knew it would be no easy task. Now that he'd seen her, Rotham understood just how difficult that task was going to be. As Charlie had reminded him with his last breath, great care must be taken to see that Georgina didn't marry the wrong man.

Still holding her hand, he said abruptly, "I don't mean to take Charles's place—no one could. But if you'll have me, I will do my best to be a brother."

Touched beyond words, the easy tears associated with Charles's loss sprang to Georgina's eyes. She moved forward, laying her forehead against his chest, leaning into the comfort of his embrace.

Rotham brought his hands up and he held her, his grip hard.

Georgina leaned against him a long moment, her cheek against his coat. Rotham heard her sniff as her weakness passed and thought she seemed embarrassed.

She raised on tiptoe to kiss his cheek before stepping away. Laughing a little, she wiped at her eyes with the back of her hand.

"I didn't mean to cry," she said and accepted the offer of his large handkerchief when he thrust it at her. "Thank you."

Her eyes were brilliant after the tears, their amber

depths lit with myriad liquid sparks. Rotham looked away. "What did you want to tell me?" he asked. "Your note said you had something to discuss."

"Yes. It was . . . I wanted to tell you my coming to town is a ruse to bring Lizzie to the notice of the ton. I've decided she needs a husband."

Rotham moved away, putting distance between them. He held his hands to the fire. "And you, Georgina? You must know a formal presentation will place you in the Marriage Mart as well." He kept his voice light with an effort.

"Oh, no!" came her casual rejoinder. "Marriage doesn't appeal to me."

His gaze was level. "You're young yet."

She nodded. "But Lizzie is twenty-two. Besides, she's domestically inclined."

"And you're not?" Rotham smiled.

Georgina's hoot of laughter was answer enough.

Two emotions warred in the earl. He felt a vast, trembling relief that Georgina wasn't set on immediate marriage and amusement that she was engaged in one of her infamous managing tricks.

He leaned his arm along the mantel, gazed down at her and asked, "What has your sister to say to this scheme of yours to catch her a husband?"

"Nothing. Lizzie doesn't know. That's what I've been wanting to tell you. That, and to ask you to support me. Will you? Colly Saltre calls it my campaign. I suppose you must be my aide-de-camp." Her eyes warmed, and laughter bubbled in her throat as she watched him expectantly.

Rotham grinned and shook his head. "You don't want an aide, Georgina. You want an accomplice."

Her face lit. "Exactly," she cried. "I knew it. I knew you wouldn't let me down."

She clapped her hands. "It's going to be such fun. Come to my study. We can be private there."

Her voice dropped to a conspirator's level. "I must tell you, Lady Romsey—whom I'd quite forgotten is your aunt—has foisted Miss Jane Postlewaite on us as a chaperone. She arrived with all her boxes from Chelsea last evening."

She opened the door and peeked out into the foyer. When the earl would have spoken, she shushed him. "Miss P. and Lizzie are just down the hall in the back parlor," she murmured.

"No, but having Miss P. won't be so bad," she continued in a stage whisper as they climbed the stairs. "At first, I didn't see any advantage in the situation. Then I realized she can be company for Lizzie when I am busy. You must know," she disclosed, as they gained the second landing, "my business takes much of my time."

"Somehow or other," Rotham said, "I'd assumed that a seventeen-year-old girl would have several trustees if she happened to be a great heiress."

The satirical nature of his comment escaped Georgina. "No, only Papa. But you know how he is. He signs whatever I put before him."

"You're joking," he said flatly.

"No, I'm not." Georgina's earnest expression confirmed his worst fears.

"But you must have a conditional guardian!" insisted Rotham.

Georgina shrugged. "No. My brother Charles was named in case Papa failed."

"Charlie is dead," Rotham reminded her bluntly. "If something happened to your father, every fortune hunter in town would beat your door down." He stopped when she smiled and shook her head.

"None of them would know how my money is left, Hugh!"

"That makes no difference. If your father should die, the Court of Chancery would step in and make you a ward. You must have another guardian immediately. Is old Peckeyham still your lawyer? He must be getting senile! Promise me, Georgina. This must be taken care of immediately!"

"I promise," she said. "Thank you. I'll invite Mr.

Peckeyham to come see Papa very soon. He can make a new will naming another trustee."

"Tomorrow," insisted Rotham.

Georgina smiled. "Tomorrow," she agreed.

They had arrived at the third landing. Georgina pushed in the door and preceded Rotham into the large chamber. He was pleased to see she left the door open without prompting.

Inviting him to sit on the deep leather sofa, Georgina slipped to the floor. She leaned her elbow on an oversized hassock and lounged on the oriental carpet.

The unconventional pose amused Rotham.

He looked about. "I like your study."

"Thank you." Georgina smiled and waited.

She seemed content to allow him to initiate further conversation or to join him in a companionable silence, he thought.

Rotham found himself wishing he could drop his guard and talk with her about whatever he wanted—this mess with Ali de Burgh, for instance.

It was apparent Georgina was relaxed. She seemed to be enjoying his company. The earl crossed his legs, determined to bring himself to grips with the impact she had on him. "Tell me about your trip from Sussex," he said. "The roads must still be covered in snow."

"Oh, yes," Georgina agreed, and they began discussing the Upcotts' journey to town, some of their mutual acquaintances, and Georgina's plans for her Season. It was in this way, during the general course of conversation, that Rotham gained a piece of information that brought him up short.

"My aunt? You don't mean to say Aunt Romsey is presenting you?" he asked in rising accents.

"Is something wrong, Hugh? Don't you approve?"

"Approve? Yes, of course. It's just . . ." In one movement he came off the sofa and strode to the fireplace.

Here was a pretty mess: He hadn't needed to go to Ali de Burgh, after all. He'd got himself into this marriage tangle for nothing!

Rotham looked into the flames as he placed his booted foot on the low fender. *Damn!*

His darkly tanned face was like flint in the reflection of the firelight. The room was rather dim, it being an overcast day with low clouds hiding the sun.

He glanced at the girl sitting on the floor. She watched him alertly, waiting to learn what bothered him. Her dark eyes were alive and interested, and he sensed her concern. Why hadn't he come to Georgina before that fateful interview? Or dropped round to discuss it with his Aunt Romsey?

Rotham gave a grunt of amusement. It wasn't funny, and yet it was. And he mustn't admit his regret at being betrothed. That would be disloyal to his future wife. He couldn't even mention his engagement to Georgina because Lady Alice didn't want it announced until Sir Percy came back to town.

The earl looked down to find amber eyes questioning him. He grinned and reached his hand to her. When she placed her slim fingers in his, he hauled Georgina up beside him.

"I was worried over nothing," he said. "I thought the task of sponsoring you had fallen on me."

Georgina gave an astonished shout of laughter. "No, you couldn't have thought that. It would have been monstrously ineligible, you know."

"Yes, I did, and it disturbed me."

"Then you must be relieved," said Georgina.

"I am. But I mean to stand by you."

"Oh, I expect it, Hugh. The Trio may dance in my train, but most of my dependence lies in you."

Rotham raised his brows in query and Georgina explained. "If anyone becomes particular in his intentions, I shall require you to hint him away."

He studied her face a long moment. "Certainly. But if you should find yourself falling in love?"

Georgina seemed to find this exquisitely amusing. She laughed, stopped, then laughed again. "I shall never marry, Hugh. I'm certain of that."

He was about to protest when she said, "Wait. Ask yourself this—who would be able to command me? Any man who married my money would never have my respect. No, only someone with his own fortune and who managed it himself could hope to influence me. I'm flagrantly independent, Hugh. I plan to legally control my estate as Mama did. Therefore, I do not contemplate matrimony. It could only lead to misery and resentment. Only imagine some poor man tied to me. Papa didn't mind with Mama, but I'm sure I'll never find a man so yielding and malleable as my dear father."

She rushed on when he would have interrupted. "In addition, I doubt the man exists who could attract me in that way. I don't precisely understand such emotions between a man and a woman. I will be frank and say I am not eager to experience those feelings. No, I'm better alone."

The earl stood with his head flung back, regarding her steadily. She is afraid of marriage, he thought. This reminded him, as nothing else, how young she actually was, how unawakened.

Georgina laid her hand on his sleeve. "Hugh? Why do you look so strange?"

"Do I? I was thinking of something else, pet. And don't be so quick to reject love. You say you don't understand it. Who does?" He touched her nose with his finger, smiled, and took his leave.

=== 7 ===

GEORGINA HAD NEVER BOXED, and she stopped wrestling with the Trio when she was eleven. But she dearly loved to fence and gave excellent account of herself after years of tutelage under Lazy.

Dressed in tightly fitting dark trousers and a white silk shirt, she presented a sight Rotham—dropping by unexpectedly—grinned to see. Laughing, her hair flying, she fenced with a furious vigor that sent her opponent's foil flying.

"Brava!" cried the earl, clapping his hands.

Georgina removed her mask, and her hair tumbled down her back. Her face was flushed and she was breathing quickly. "Hugh!" she exclaimed. She came to him and offered her hand. "I didn't know you were here. Were you watching?"

"You said to come anytime," Rotham reminded her. He looked at her lovely mouth smiling brightly at him. He found himself wanting to touch her hair, and dropped her hand when he could. The trousers she was dressed in, he thought, were damned attractive. He was glad no other man could see her; he didn't count the Trio.

Later, dressed more conventionally in her riding habit, Georgina sat at the round table off the herb garden and ate as heartily as the Trio.

Mrs. Mucklesby, face beaming, clucked over the group like a mother hen. She insisted that the earl, who had already eaten and refused to join the feast, at least have a cup of tea.

"Another time, Mrs. Mucklesby." He watched the cook blush with pleasure at his remembering her name.

It was a pleasant group that visited the kitchens, Rotham thought as the boys and Georgina dug in. Lizzie and Colly drifted in and casually served themselves from the sideboard.

"You've quite a colony here," Rotham remarked, looking about.

They laughed and Georgina said, "But that's perfect. Shall we adopt Hugh's idea and call ourselves the 'Kitchen Colony'?" Everyone agreed, and Georgina said it was all settled. "We love to eat here," she told him. "Isn't it nice? And it saves dear Hutchins the trouble of transporting all this to the dining room." She waved at the heavily laden table.

Rotham saw Mrs. Mucklesby smile as she listened to Georgina. It was obvious she adored the girl.

Who could help adoring Georgina? he asked himself.

Those first days in London passed in an exciting whirl for Georgina. The Trio drove her and Lizzie to Bond Street and they bought mounds of clothes. Dressed as a boy, Georgina drove the Silver Cloud on Hampstead Heath.

She gave a small dinner party with Lady Romsey and Sir Graham as guests, and when Sir Graham took Georgina to dine in the city, she found herself in the company of those men, cits and peers alike, who controlled the power and wealth of London and, by extension, the world.

Lizzie exclaimed when Georgina had her hair cut in front. But Georgina said, "No, Lizzie. Don't you see? This gives me short curls here." She fluffed the hair over her forehead and crown. "And it leaves the sides and back long for braids or twists when I have my hair put up."

In her own rooms, she left her hair loose and swinging around her shoulders. It reached almost to her waist in back.

Rotham liked to watch Georgina as she sat on the floor, arguing and laughing with the Trio. She included him freely in all their ripping conversations, and when she disagreed with him, denounced his views as readily as she did the Trio's.

In spite of his good intentions, Rotham found himself in Upper Brook Street each day, alone or with a friend. He looked forward to his first sight of Georgina.

His consolation was that she was so young she had no inkling how he felt about her. She looked on him as a friend and adviser; the earl was determined that she continue. He kept a little aloof, laughing and teasing her, refusing to fence when she demanded it. He rarely touched her, making certain no action of his would give Georgina reason to suspect his true feelings.

Alone in his library, gazing into the fire, Rotham concluded there was nothing he could do about Georgina and deliberately turned his mind to his fiancée. He was interrupted by the entrance of Fen.

His friend came lounging into the library and cast himself onto the settee. "Just dropped by," he announced. "Knew I wouldn't be seeing you tonight."

The earl opened his eyes at his friend. "Are you going out of town?" he asked.

"Not at all," Fenshaw said, yawning hugely. "Knew you wouldn't be coming to the little Ruxton's party this evening."

"Why not?" Rotham asked, his teeth setting hard. He didn't care a pin for Maxine Ruxton or any of the demimonde, but his resentment at his predicament was choking him.

Fenshaw lifted his brows and stared silently at the earl a long moment. Shrugging, he said, "I thought you must be having dinner with your intended every evening."

Rotham frowned. Had Alice expected him to come to Berkeley Square to dine at night? She'd said nothing.

When his friend left, Rotham got himself into his coat and made his way to Bruton Street.

But dinner with her betrothed, as Rotham discovered, was the farthest thing from Lady Alice's mind.

She gave him her hand. "I'm sorry, Hugh. As you can see, I'm dressed to go out. A meeting of the Committee for Unwed Mothers. I wasn't expecting you, but you're welcome to dine with Papa any night you drop around. I make it a point to eat with him on Thursdays and Sundays. Was there anything in particular you wanted?"

His relief that he wasn't expected to sit in his fiancée's pocket put Hugh quite in charity with her. "No. You said nothing and I wondered if I should . . . if I must . . . but if you're busy, that leaves me free to . . ."

Lady Alice smiled. "Don't change your plans a jot for me. I'm an independent woman; very busy, always on the go. You said you wouldn't mind my continuing as I am."

Rotham shook his head. "Not at all. That takes a great load off my mind. I mean . . ."

"We'll have a comfortable marriage, Hugh. I'm sure of it." Alice patted his arm absently. Her thoughts, Rotham suspected, were already on her meeting.

Rotham was relieved Lady Alice had deferred the announcement of their engagement until Sir Percy returned to London. When the situation was known, everyone in the ton would surely wonder why he spent so much time at Upcott House and in the company of Georgina Upcott.

He couldn't claim to be Georgina's guardian or warden; the excuse of friendship with her dead brother was a trifle thin. His continued visits would cause talk and that mustn't happen. When the world knew he was a betrothed man, he must concentrate on Lady Alice. He felt impelled to spend every possible moment with Georgina before Alice decided to make their alliance known, for he expected Sir Percy back at any time.

When Rotham arrived at Upcott House the next morning, he found a little scene going forward in the hall. Miss Postlewaite, Lizzie, and Colly were confronting Georgina, who seemed to be demanding something they weren't prepared to yield.

He saw that they were all dressed to go out. Georgina, Rotham thought, was ravishing in a long plum-colored double-breasted redingote, very tightly fitted and trimmed with sable. She wore a sable hat and carried a huge muff of the same dark fur. Her eyes were flashing brilliantly—with anger, he suspected—and he thought he'd never seen her so beautiful or desirable.

"Hugh!" she greeted him abruptly, giving him her small gloved hand. "Will you tell these two that it looks singular for them to travel about London together?"

Rotham bit his lip to keep from smiling.

Lizzie blushed and dropped her eyes.

Colly, natty in a caped great-coat, held his low-crowned beaver by his side and looked conscious.

Rotham shook hands with the gentleman and looked at Georgina. "Playing propriety, are we?"

Georgina did not seem to appreciate his attempt at humor. Her eyes snapped to his and she raised her brows.

"Not very successfully. Miss P. says she must go with me into the city. She has taken it into her head that my dining with Sir Graham and his associates will compromise me and throw me into who-knows-what kind of company. I have explained that I shall take Gilly—my maid, you know—as I did last time. Miss P. can then go with Lizzie and Colly."

Rotham caught Miss Postlewaite's gaze. She shook her head slightly and rolled her eyes toward the ceiling. He grinned understandingly.

"Why don't I escort Georgina into the city?" he asked Jane. "That will leave you free to accompany Miss Upcott and Lord Saltre wherever they wish to go."

He turned to find Georgina smiling broadly. "The very thing, Hugh. I'm sure Sir Graham won't mind your coming. But hurry. We mustn't delay. I have my carriage waiting."

As they rolled away from Upcott House, Georgina said quickly, "Rotham, thank you. The ton mustn't get the idea that Colly is courting Lizzie. Her chances would plummet to zero if anyone should think, ridiculous though it may be, that there is an understanding between them."

Rotham nodded and glanced at the little maid sitting beside Georgina.

"Oh," said Georgina, patting Gilly's hand. "Gilly is totally trustworthy. She knows all my plans to catch Lizzie a husband. I rely on her absolutely. Gilly, say hello to Lord Rotham. Rotham, this is Gilly Driggers from East Anglia."

Rotham smiled and acknowledged the young maid's greeting.

"My lord," she said, nodding gravely.

Then she looked out the window, succeeding, he thought, in nearly making herself invisible.

To keep his mind off Georgina's perfume, he asked, "Where in the city are we going?"

"Just off Fleet Street," Georgina replied.

Rotham stiffened as they turned down a mean and narrow side street. "I see what Miss Postlewaite meant, Georgina. This is no place for you to be traveling alone."

He would have said more, but Gilly Driggers gave a small shriek and cried, "Miss Georgina! Look there! It's Jack Haggman from the village. It's a press gang, miss. They're taking poor Jack up for sure! Oh, can't you do something?"

"Certainly," Georgina said calmly. She thumped on the roof with her parasol.

"Stop the carriage," she called, pulling the drawstring on her muff.

"You're not going into the street?" Rotham demanded. He laid a restraining hand on her arm.

Georgina brushed aside his objection. "I must rescue Gilly's friend, Hugh. I should think the sergeant would welcome a friendly donation to his favorite charity." She smiled and opened her gloved hand. On her palm lay five golden guineas.

Rotham, furious that Georgina had been about to step

into danger, shoved the money back at her. "Wait here; I shall return with—what's his name?" This last was directed at the maid.

"Jack Haggman, sir. Oh, please hurry! They're milling poor Jack down; he's too stubborn to give up. They'll kill him!"

Rotham left the coach with a last admonition. "Georgina, I mean it. Stay inside."

"Hugh! Take this," she said and shoved a small pistol at him. "You might need it." She had produced the gun from the depths of her muff.

He drew a ragged sigh. "Georgina," he breathed softly, "we shall discuss that weapon you're carrying in the very near future. We shall discuss it at length. We shall also address the question of what would have happened had I not been with you today."

Without another word he dropped to the pavement and advanced upon the scuffling men in the dark shadows, his hand in the pocket of his overcoat. In a very short time he returned, trailed by a husky country lad.

Rotham threw open the door of the carriage. "Here is your prize, Gilly. I've sent for a jarvey."

Turning to Georgina, he said, "I trust you had some purpose in mind when you set out to rescue this person." Rotham's tone was curt. He couldn't help it.

Georgina, eyes flashing, said, "Of course. Jack shall be employed as a groom. Do you know anything about horses, Jack?"

"Thank you, miss. Was raised on a farm, I was. I'm a rare hand with horses, miss."

The hack that Rotham ordered arrived, and he put Gilly and Jack into it and sent them to Upper Brook Street. Then he climbed into the carriage to face a defiant Georgina.

Rotham clenched his fists on his thighs to keep from reaching for her. He closed his eyes a moment. Scenes of her being roughly handled flashed before his inner vision, and he felt himself break into a cold sweat. He opened his eyes and found her looking at him with concern.

"Hugh?" she asked, her voice small. "Are you all right?"

He settled back into his seat. The carriage was moving again.

Rotham removed his hat and wiped his brow with his handkerchief. He ran his fingers through his hair and reseated his hat on his head. Only then did he look fully at the girl across from him.

"Georgina," he said, "I've never told you what Charlie's last words were, have I?"

She seemed puzzled. Shaking her head, she said, "N— no."

Rotham's voice was calm and controlled, very low. "His last thoughts were of you. We were in the snow and he knew he was dying. He asked me to watch after you, Georgina. I don't think I've done a very good job. Why else would you feel constrained to carry a pistol? I'm sure Charlie would disapprove."

Georgina gave a great sob and hid her face in her hands.

Rotham didn't dare touch her. He let her cry. He knew she was suffering, but she must realize that she couldn't go into dangerous places or into situations where she thought she might need a weapon.

"That gun you're carrying, Georgina. You can't imagine how it feels to kill someone. I've killed more men than I care to remember. At night, sometimes, I see their faces. War is horrible, Georgina. When you kill a man, you watch his life drain from him, his soul slip away. He seems to shrink before your eyes. He becomes a loathsome, pitiful thing, fit only for a cold grave."

Georgina was watching him, listening to his soft words, tears sliding down her cheeks. Rotham gave her his handkerchief.

"I—I want to go home, Hugh. Will you send a message to Sir Graham? And will you take the gun? I'm sorry. The Trio and I like to cup wafers." She hiccupped on a long sob. "I'm quite good, you know. I'll never carry the gun again. I promise; you have my word."

Rotham smiled. "That's good, sweetheart. I know you won't break a promise. Keep the gun and put it away when you get home. That's a good girl."

The trouble, Rotham told himself later, was that Georgina was just a girl. He kept seeing her as a woman, and he wanted her more than he'd ever wanted anyone in his life.

He formed the intention of staying away, but found he couldn't.

Alone in Georgina's study—long after the Trio left—they talked for hours, exploring personalities, opinions, likes and dislikes.

Rotham told her of his early life spent with his grandfather, of the trips he and the old earl had taken to Greece and Egypt, and how his grandfather had taught him to love exploring the ruins.

"What I want to do now," Rotham told her one night, "is investigate the old Celtic fields on Windmill Hill in Hampshire."

"Oh, yes!" Georgina cried, going up on her knees in excitement. As usual she was on the floor, leaning against her favorite hassock. "I wish I could go with you. Rocks are all very well; Papa's work is certainly important. But, at least for me, what people have done in ages past seems much more important, more vital somehow, than the study of rock formations which have been crumbling since time began. There's no comparison. Only consider Stonehenge, Hugh. When I saw it, all I could think of, staring at those gigantic boulders, was that some ancient people had done it; men had conceived of the *plan* of moving those great monoliths to that place and arranging them according to their own design. What an undertaking. And who knows for what purpose? And then we have Hadrian's Wall! We know why it's there. It was a military project and shows what men can do when some general or king decides to build something. Oh! Do you realize how much I envy you, Hugh? I'd love to explore the wonders of the world. But Society wouldn't countenance my going alone. Only think what Lizzie and your Aunt Romsey would say. See? Even your face changed when I mentioned it. Never mind. I don't think I'd enjoy it without sharing it with someone as interested in it as I am."

Georgina begged Rotham to bring his camp journals so she could see them, and when he appeared one night with a large portfolio of his notes under his arm, they spent hours going over his jottings and drawings.

"Why do you start digging in so many places, Hugh?"

"Because I can only see the bit of ground I'm standing on and have to guess where to start. Sometimes, when I can climb to high ground and there aren't trees in the way, I can enjoy a better prospective."

The fire in the study burned to embers and the candles were guttering in their sockets. Neither of them noticed.

Rotham watched Georgina settle herself amongst the maps and charts spread on the floor. At that moment, the clock struck two. He indicated that he should leave, but Georgina shook her head and motioned for him to remain seated, that she wasn't ready for him to go.

"Because I want to tell you something I've just thought of, Hugh. What you need is a bird's-eye view."

He watched Georgina as she pushed back her hair. Rotham knew he would always remember this moment, alone with her at this witching hour. She nibbled her lip, totally unself-conscious, sublimely unaware how appealing she was in her tousled, sleepy-eyed state. His sense of loss was so acute he turned away and began rolling his charts.

Georgina jumped to her feet and grabbed his arm. "No, but only listen, Hugh. I've had one of my revelations. It's very simple. You must hire one of those hot-air balloons. You can fly directly over the old Celtic farms and see what you make of the situation. You'd know exactly where to dig."

Rotham stopped gathering his papers and looked at Georgina in astonishment. "My God, I think you're right. If only I could."

"But what's stopping you?" she asked, throwing her arms wide.

"I'll look into tomorrow," he grinned. "And if this works, I'll fly over Hambledon Hill, Dorset. There's an ancient hilltop camp there. Thanks for the idea, brat."

This was Charlie's favorite nickname for her, and Georgina's eyes misted, hearing it on Rotham's lips. She looked at him with tears hanging on her lashes. "Hugh. Let's never change. Promise we'll always be the good friends we are right now."

═ 8 ═

WHEN GEORGINA WENT in search of Lizzie the next morning, she found her, as usual, with Colly Saltre in the yellow parlour.

"Georgina," Colly said, "we are visiting Lord Wolford this morning. His lordship has asked Lord Rotham and me to help him erect this famous battle, you see. Won't you come along?"

"I'd like that," Georgina replied without hesitation. "I've been meaning to look at Lord Wolford's battles."

"You may not know," Lizzie said, smiling proudly at her kinsman, "that Colly has been in correspondence with his lordship for years."

Colly waved a large hand. "Yes. Been writing to Lord Wolford a long time. Always wanted to visit him, but circumstances prevented it, you see, and the press of duties in Northumberland. All that."

Georgina nodded her understanding.

"Now I've finally met Lord Wolford and he has kindly promised to let me help," Colly said. "Lots of work there: setting up the diorama, checking details of the battle; I may even be painting lead soldiers. No job too large or small, too insignificant or minute, but what I'll be happy to lend my hand."

Georgina and Lizzie were settled in Colly's coach when the Trio arrived in the Silver Cloud. Georgina leaned out the window and told them where they were headed.

"We'll come, too," Tessie yelled from the box. "Dexter

has to run in for the muffins Mrs. Mucklesby promised him. Go along; we'll follow."

It was quite a group that Benton escorted up the long staircase at Wolford House. Georgina had never been there before and looked about with interest.

They found Lord Wolford on the floor with his knees on a pillow, holding a measuring stick. He stood for introductions, clearly distracted at the interruption, but pleased when he discovered who they were and that they had come to see and help with his battle.

"Haven't got it going yet," his lordship told Colly. "Only just now laying out the grid; have to get it all in the proper perspective and scale."

He gestured to two easels in a corner of the room. "Those are drawings of the retreat to Corunna, and the battle itself. Rotham suggested I do it; he was wounded in this battle, you know."

The earl walked in just in time to see Lizzie press her handkerchief to her mouth. He stopped to whisper something to the young footman and crossed to her. "This must be painful for you, Miss Upcott. I'm sorry you came."

Mercifully, Lady Alice arrived just then, summoned by the footman. Her voice overrode Rotham's. "I'm so sorry," she said, putting her arm about Lizzie's shoulders. "This reminds you of the loss of your brother; we wouldn't have you upset for anything in the world."

But Lizzie had conquered her weak moment. She looked about for Georgina. "I'm fine now, but my sister. Please don't let her see this."

Georgina, who had heard everything, cast a look at Hugh and said in a steely little voice, "Show me where Charlie was killed." She walked to the easels and Rotham followed.

"I can't. This isn't the scene where it happened. Here, we were fighting a rearguard action and being loaded aboard the transports."

He looked down at her. Georgina's lips were white and one corner of her mouth trembled.

After a moment, she cleared her throat and tried to smile.

"I am sure you've been a great help to Lord Wolford in all this, Hugh."

It was an easy excuse for his presence at Wolford House, Rotham thought. He was tempted to say nothing, to put off awhile what he'd been dreading to tell Georgina.

He had opened his mouth to inform her of his betrothal when Lady Alice came forward and grasped his arm.

"It's not generally known, Georgina, but Rotham and I are engaged." Lady Alice smiled. "We've agreed to say nothing until Colonel Milhouse returns to town."

Rotham noticed that Lizzie had come to stand beside her sister. He kept his eyes on Georgina, who jerked up her head at Lady Alice's words.

"I . . . I'm sure you'll keep our secret until then," Alice said.

Rotham thought Georgina's silence was a little over-drawn. His eyes narrowed. Did she look pale?

Lizzie, her pleasure evident, said, "My very best wishes to you both. How exciting. We won't say a word."

Georgina gave Rotham and Alice a long cool look, then glanced away.

Rotham felt Alice lift her head sharply. He looked at her and saw that she was flushing.

Georgina's expression baffled him. Her congratulations were somewhat delayed and consisted of polite nothings. She flashed him another strange look, and he almost grinned. He thought he understood. Managing minx. She was angry because she wasn't in on the secret.

After everyone left, Alice tried to explain herself to Rotham. "I cannot think why I told them our news," she remarked. "It just popped out, and that's not like me."

The earl shrugged. "Bound to come out sooner or later. Then everyone will know."

"Why hadn't you told Miss Georgina Upcott?" Alice asked.

"You were the one who declined to let me put it in the papers," he said in a bored way. "Don't worry; the

Upcott girls won't spread it about until you formally announce it."

Alice shot a quick glance at Rotham, hesitated, and said with a laugh, "I'd have sworn the younger one was jealous when I told them. What have you done to make her fall in love with you?"

Hugh's frown was quick and his hand, raising a pinch of snuff, was suddenly arrested. "You're joking. She's little more than a child."

He sounded harsher than Alice had ever heard him. "Well, of course I'm joking, Hugh," she said in a lighter tone, her manner teasing. "What I can't understand is why you were almost laughing at the poor girl."

The earl relaxed and smiled. "Georgina likes to be in on everything. She was angry because I hadn't taken her into my confidence."

"Oh." Lady Alice's brow cleared. "But are you sure she won't spread it about? Some people can't keep from displaying what they've learned about others, especially if it's a secret. She is very young."

"Not Georgina. She has a stout little heart and a true one. You could tell her anything."

That was the longest night of Georgina's life. She dressed for bed; she turned the covers back. She even slipped under the comforter awhile. But in the end, she walked the floor of her study until dawn broke over Mayfair, the rooftops glistening with the sheen of frost coating their edges.

She relived the moment Lady Alice made her disastrous announcement. In that fleeting instant, Georgina knew she was in love with Rotham and couldn't have him.

As the hours crept by she remembered every word he had ever spoken to her, every look he had given her. Methodically, she took her life apart. Georgina reached the conclusion that her original plan had been good. She had come to town to get Lizzie a husband, to take her own place in Society and to bring her father close to his publishers. And, after all, she had never wanted to marry, so perhaps it was for the best.

Angrily she brushed at the tears wetting her face. If she couldn't have the earl any other way, she would settle for his friendship. And that, though Georgina disliked the idea, meant cultivating the acquaintance of Lady Alice de Burgh.

The sun peeped over the horizon in that instant, sending its brilliant beams straight into her bedchamber.

Georgina drew a deep breath and braced herself. Rotham must never know she loved him. Not that way. Let him know she loved him as a friend, as a brother, as a confidant. Let him know she leaned on him, cherished him, and wished him all of life's happiness. But never let him know how she longed to be held, that she dreamed of his kisses.

Georgina whirled from the window, calling for her maid. She would have a bath and dress in her new blue riding habit.

"And the hat with the long black feather, Gilly. Give me that."

She would take Sultan on a wild run through the park. She wanted the sleek muscles bunching under her, the animal's fine will bent to her command. She wanted the morning breeze in her face. She would race the wind down Rotten Row and damn what anyone thought.

The earl greeted the same dawn with a sense of resignation. He was aware that secret news travels fast, and since he didn't want his Aunt Romsey to hear about his engagement from anyone except himself, went to tell her about it. He was too late. Lady Romsey had it via Miss Postlewaite in a message delivered to her breakfast table.

She was not pleased. Upon the earl's appearance, she stamped her foot and rang a peal over his head. "I can't believe you've done such a stupid thing, Hugh. And now, Georgina has come. The girl would be perfect for you," she cried. "She's lively, intelligent, and beginning to show great beauty. Just the sort of wife to keep you interested. And she likes you; I could see that when we all met in the park last week. You've never enjoyed simpering misses and Georgina certainly isn't that. She's perfect. And now you've ruined everything by getting engaged to Alice de Burgh."

Rotham flinched. He recovered quickly, but a sense of yearning possessed him and his aunt looked at him with a dawning expression.

"Oh, you poor boy. You're in love with her already, aren't you? And engaged to Lady Alice."

At any other time, his aunt's intuitive guess would have amused Rotham. Now he only wanted to check such a rumor before it started. To protest too much would be fatal.

"No, no, Aunt Olivia. Georgina is a dear, but you know how I feel about girls in their first Season. They bore me to tears. They're too young to have formed any sort of character, and they giggle and gush and spout lines their mamas have taught them."

"I know what it is," Lady Romsey interrupted. "You can't see how beautiful she is and that she'll only grow more so."

Not see? thought Rotham. A man would be blind not to see the beauty in Georgina.

"On the contrary," he said mildly. "I think Georgina looks very well. In fact, she's quite pretty. But I remember her as a child of eleven. To my mind, seventeen isn't much older. Too many raw emotions there. No, Alice and I will rub on very well together. Neither of us is looking for love in marriage. Alice can give me children, and she can help with Georgina."

"Georgina will be eighteen in a few weeks," Lady Romsey pointed out.

Rotham pretended to stifle a yawn. "There's very little difference in seventeen and eighteen." He shrugged and turned their conversation to other matters.

In an effort to reassure himself about his coming marriage, the earl went to dine with Lady Alice and Lord Wolford on Thursday.

Wolford House was comfortable and Alice ran it with a precision that must please, Rotham thought. But he found he wasn't in any mood to be pleased. He could see himself enduring a dismal succession of Thursdays, talking with old Wolford about his battles. Like a child, Lord Wolford was single-minded. He couldn't get his mind off his lead soldiers. When the meal was over, he wandered back up to his war room, and Rotham was left alone with Lady Alice.

He wondered if she'd withdraw, leaving him to drink a solitary glass of port before joining him, but she stayed scribbling on the lists she had carried in to dinner. When he expressed interest, she told him the lists concerned her charities or various social events. "I always work on them at the table, Hugh."

The earl sipped his tea. "Seems to keep you busy," he commented.

"Yes," Alice said.

Rotham nodded. They had very little to discuss when it came to charities or Society doings. Alice knew his view on those.

Remembering his wonderful conversations with Georgina about digging, Rotham thought Alice might like to hear about them. He began to speak of what he'd been doing the past few years and what he planned for the future.

"You will enjoy going to Greece and Turkey, Ali. It's wonderful, roughing it, living in a tent, far from people. It's delightful to get away from everything and simply let the world slide," he assured her, ignoring the skeptical expression that flitted across her face.

"Besides," he said, warming to his subject, "one never knows what ancient artifacts one might be lucky enough to find."

Lady Alice smiled and said lightly, "That might be true, but I'm afraid I can't imagine myself leaving London for some dreary camp in the wilds of Greece or Turkey. Fighting flies in some dusty place hundreds of miles from civilization isn't at all to my taste. I know you enjoy it;

you must go anytime you please. But really, Hugh, you can't expect me to like such things, or even understand why anyone would wish to go. I'm certain archaeology is interesting enough if one cares for that sort of thing, but I find myself unable to appreciate the exploration of antiquities as I ought. Such ruins have remained hidden under dirt and rubble hundreds of years. What good does it do to uncover them now?"

While Rotham tried to think of something to say, Alice continued in the same vein. "I can see," she told him, "that hobbies, if one needs such things to fill one's time, are useful enough. My father whiles away many otherwise dull hours with his toy soldiers and genealogical research. As for me, my dear Hugh, I am far too busy to waste time that way." She smiled. "And if, in the future, you should decide to put your spare time to some *practical* use, I'll be delighted to have you join me in my work."

Rotham went away certain he and Lady Alice would never have anything in common except their children. Theirs was destined to be the usual marriage of two strangers in the same unhappy household, he thought.

Perversely, he blamed Georgina for his unhappy state. If Georgina hadn't made him fall in love with her, Rotham decided, he wouldn't be so dissatisfied with Alice. Knowing Georgina, being with her these past few days, had made him aware of just how much he wanted a wife he could love and laugh with.

Rotham forced himself to stay away for two days; then he realized his anger was hurting no one except himself. And what would she think if he no longer visited in Brook Street?

Rotham wondered if the news of his engagement had shaken Georgina as much as Alice thought. He supposed it was possible that she had developed a girlish *tendre* for him.

He thought he had successfully hidden his own feelings. If he continued to hide them, Georgina would accept that there could only be friendship between them and he would marry Alice de Burgh and forget golden eyes and long auburn hair with silken glints.

To his relief, Rotham's next meeting with Georgina was without incident. He had formed the habit of visiting informally after dinner when he knew the family had no engagements. He called one evening, knowing that even if Georgina were out, his stopping by would show nothing had changed.

Hutchins bowed the earl in and informed him what various inhabitants of the house were doing: Miss Elizabeth and Miss Postlewaite were still out with Mr. Saltre, visiting some of the gentleman's friends in Chelsea. Sir Owen had decided to work on the book again. Miss Georgina and the Trio were engaged in a heavy game of chance in her study. "Would your lordship care to be shown up?" Hutchins asked.

His lordship would. He entered Georgina's private domain to find the betting lively and the stakes beans.

Rotham looked at Georgina, expertly shuffling the cards, and his face relaxed. She'd thrown him a quick smile and continued arguing with Tessie over some point in the game. She seemed exactly as she always was.

He stayed only a few minutes. When she saw that he was leaving, she called, "I'll see you tomorrow, Hugh."

He was glad Georgina was taking his engagement to Lady Alice in stride, Rotham told himself. He climbed into his carriage and settled back. Maybe he could sleep easier tonight. But a wave of regret suddenly swept over him. He wished to God the Upcotts had never come to town.

═ 9 ═

GEORGINA KNEW THAT if she stayed busy, she'd have less time to think. In spite of the bitterly cold weather, the next few days found her in a feverish whirl of activity.

She ordered her household and settled in the two new members who had come into her service that second week in town.

Georgina had been drawn to Gilly Driggers from the first interview. The girl was an excellent maid and dresser. When Gilly disclosed that her sister Mattie had disappeared from her place of service in Piccadilly, Georgina told the girl that she would help her locate the missing Mattie if they had to search all summer.

The grateful Jack Haggman, after his rescue from the press gang, swore to serve Georgina always. She revised her original plan, and rather than make him a groom, appointed him her personal footman—and bodyguard.

With Gilly in the carriage playing abigail and Jack riding on the step, Georgina went all over London, and everywhere they went they looked for the errant sister.

Georgina patronized Child's Bank, located next to Temple Bar in Fleet Street. She visited in the city with Sir Graham Bardolph and captivated his circle of business friends. She asked her solicitor, Mr. Peckeyham, to Upcott House to add a codicil to Papa's will.

Rotham was pleased when she told him Sir Graham and Mr. Theobald Hexter, a business acquaintance of her mother's, were added as her new trustees.

Georgina took her father's manuscript to Paternoster Row and had her portrait painted in miniature by Mr. Henry Bone. Giving herself no time to dwell on her feelings for Rotham, she traveled to Bunhill Row, the old Quaker section, in search of antiques. She saw to her rental properties in Sloan Street and down by Blackfriars Bridge. At Gillows, she shopped for new furniture. She dragged Lizzie to the smartest couturiers in Bond Street and was forced to take Colly along when her sister refused to go without him.

Georgina's evenings were just as crowded. At Carlton House she was informed by Mr. Creevey of all the latest scandals. She met Samuel Rogers at Holland House; they discussed finance. She looked up to find Rotham glaring at her and later had to endure a lecture on the impropriety of a young girl in such a notorious place.

"And Carlton House, too," Rotham scolded. "First that den of iniquity and now this. If you want to please me, Georgina, you will not accept such invitations again. And the Trio should know better than to have brought you."

"I hadn't realized that pleasing you must be an ambition of mine," Georgina drawled, pushing back the bright core of anger she felt.

Rotham did exactly what he pleased—got himself engaged, for instance. She glanced at his hard face and looked away. Who knew what other heedless things, what disreputable company he indulged in? And yet *she* was supposed to toe a line of his marking? Georgina thought not.

"As for the Trio, don't go blaming them," Georgina said coolly. "They wouldn't bring me. Gregory Mandiford did. Lizzie and I were dining with Sir Graham and Gregory was there. Gregory mentioned he was coming this way and offered to drop us home. When we got to Park Lane, I said I wanted to see Holland House. We let Lizzie out, took up Gilly, and came on."

Georgina grinned at Rotham's lowering expression. "Don't worry. Gregory is such a nodcock he probably doesn't know it's improper for me to be here."

"But *you* knew."

Georgina shrugged and waved to Lord Holland. Their genial host, short and fat in his formal black, waved back, smiling with his own brand of charm. "Yes. But I knew you wouldn't bring me, so I came when I had the chance."

"Georgina," he growled.

Eyes glinting, Georgina laid her hand on his sleeve. "Don't worry, Hugh. I won't do it again." Like the naughty child who has already eaten the forbidden sweets, she was ready to be good.

"Brat," he smiled and locked his fingers around her bare wrist.

Georgina gasped at the effect of his touch on her. If she was to keep her vow to win Rotham's friendship, she must never let him touch her again. No, that's impossible, she thought. She must brace herself in the future for the electric shock his hard grip had given her.

Luckily Rotham dropped her wrist at that moment and the warm sensation left her flesh. Georgina raised her eyes to his. "Was it really so bad, Hugh?"

He grinned. "Yes. Both houses are full of aging old roués just waiting to eat beautiful girls like you. Did Gregory Mandiford take you to Carlton House, too?"

"No," Georgina smiled. "Colly Saltre did. When Lizzie said perhaps we shouldn't go, Colly assured us that nothing could be said so long as we were under his protection."

"That clunch," Rotham swore. "Thinks he's up to every rig in town. Ten to one he doesn't know what a reputation the Regent's crowd has."

"No," Georgina said. "I don't suppose he does. Colly has already made up his mind about everything in the world; he wouldn't appreciate my trying to change it."

"Unworthy, Georgina," Rotham told her. "You knew you and Lizzie shouldn't be at Carlton House. If you won't think of yourself, think of the consequences to her reputation. You'll never get her respectably married if it's known she has become one of the Carlton House crowd."

But the notion of her staid sister in such fast company

was too much for Georgina. She threw back her head and laughed up at him.

Rotham merely smiled, looking down at her with half-closed eyes. "I'm taking you home," he said.

Georgina looked in her mirror that night. Beautiful girls like you, Rotham had said. She gazed at her reflection. Her features seemed exactly the same, but if he thought she was beautiful, she was glad.

Accompanied by Jane, Lizzie, and Colly, Georgina arrived in Bruton Street at ten the next morning. She was carrying a gift for Lord Wolford.

The old man was delighted. "Lead soldiers, my dear? One can never have enough!"

Alice must be called down to admire the gift, then she and Lizzie retired to the morning room for a cup of tea while Georgina made Lord Wolford happy by hanging on to his every word concerning his forthcoming battle.

It was then that Georgina had one of her brilliant inspirations.

"Why not set up large tables at waist height, my lord? Build your battles on them and you needn't kneel on a pillow on the floor. Also," she smiled as another idea popped into her fertile brain, "why not appropriate a whole *series* of rooms, setting up tables and scenes in each one? You needn't take them down so soon. Or ever. You could show different stages of each battle. That would make them even more interesting. You could turn the whole house into a war museum."

Lord Wolford recognized a good notion when he heard one. He promptly invited Georgina to tour the house with him and select a suite of rooms. As they settled on a suite near the portrait gallery, he said, "And I expect your help, my dear. Come anytime with Saltre; he and Rotham have promised they will come every day."

Georgina smiled and said she expected Lord Wolford should be seeing her in Bruton Street quite often. She smiled even more broadly when Lady Alice reinforced her father's invitation.

Once she had accepted the fact that the Battle of Corunna, or the Retreat, was where Charles was killed, Georgina enjoyed working on Lord Wolford's project. She came almost every morning and brought Lizzie, for a comfortable little friendship had sprung up between her sister and Lady Alice. Lizzie didn't help with the battle; she assisted Alice with her charity work.

"I'm glad you and Lady Alice go on so well, Lizzie," Georgina said. "At least you don't spend so much time with Colly. He must be discouraged from sitting in your pocket. Whatever is wrong? Why do you look that way? You know it's true. I'm sorry, but I find Colly a dead bore." They had arrived at Wolford House, and Georgina ignored her sister's surreptitious use of her handkerchief as they descended from the carriage. It was time Lizzie was forced to see someone besides Colly Saltre.

Georgina had fallen into this close association with the de Burghs so she could be near Rotham, and she saw him every day. He and Sir Percy—since the colonel's return to town—were Lord Wolford's military advisers.

On the morning when Lizzie excitedly read the formal announcement of Rotham's betrothal, Georgina could accept the public fact with a measure of tolerance and acquitted herself very well when she came to Wolford House.

She was already at work with the colonel, arranging the scene where Moore was killed, when Rotham arrived.

Colly gravely extended his hand and congratulated the earl.

The colonel, after a strange grim look, did the same, and Georgina quietly offered her best wishes. She was sincere in this. If Rotham couldn't love her, then she hoped he could find happiness with Lady Alice.

Georgina turned to the colonel when Rotham went upstairs to speak to his betrothed. "You've known Rotham and Lady Alice a long time, haven't you, sir?"

Sir Percy nodded, reseating himself at the table where they were working. "Yes. The earl was in my command,

and when I came home wounded, I found Lady Alice working closely with my sister Hannah on their charities. Since my sister's death, Alice has served on the Milhouse Trust with me."

"You seem to have been close to your sister. You must miss her very much," Georgina remarked, wondering why he'd never married.

The colonel shifted in his chair. "I do, but I have much to do; I see Lady Alice every day. She has been my mainstay. We are . . . good friends," he said.

Georgina opened her eyes at his tone. He seemed pensive, and she wondered if he hadn't felt sorrow when Lady Alice became engaged to Rotham.

"I'm sure Lady Alice's marriage to Rotham won't curtail her charitable work. If fact, she said something to that effect last evening when she and Miss P. took Lizzie and me to the opera."

The colonel drew a long breath. "I'm sure she and Rotham are excellently suited. It's the best thing for both of them." He smiled at Georgina, but the smile did not reach his eyes.

It's almost as if he were in love with Lady Alice, Georgina thought. Later, she dismissed the idea as a by-product of her own yearnings.

As the days passed, Georgina found the colonel most amiable. She decided that her imagination, always overactive, had led her to suspect Sir Percy of harboring a *tendre* for Lady Alice.

Georgina's cousin completed Lord Wolford's team, the rest of the Trio having shabbed off. Dex was in charge of painting uniforms on the lead soldiers. He enjoyed this and sat for hours meticulously dabbing at the miniature figures.

She and Rotham collaborated on a papier-mâché mountain for the rugged terrain. As they set it in place, the earl remarked, "Your lightest wish seems to be Lord Wolford's command, Georgina; I only beg you won't suggest that his lordship bring in huge tanks of water to represent the Atlantic Ocean."

His smile faded when Georgina pretended to give this serious thought. When she grinned, he lightly tapped her chin. "Brat," he murmured, and she wondered how his touch could heal and hurt at the same time.

Lady Alice and Lizzie walked in at that moment, and Georgina turned away. She had noticed that Alice invariably walked to Rotham's side and stood with her arm linked in his, as if proclaiming to the world her possession.

"Hugh," Alice said, "Lizzie and I've been talking about getting up a theater party later this week. Shall we set a night?"

At the theatre, Georgina found herself seated in front of Rotham in his box. Lady Alice sat in front of the colonel.

Alice had directed the seating, and Georgina thought she saw a glance pass between Lady Romsey and Miss Postlewaite at the arrangements.

Georgina watched Alice murmur in the colonel's ear all through the first act. She was aware of Rotham behind her.

Coming home from the theater, Rotham dropped Lady Alice in Bruton Street and took Sir Percy home. His carriage drew up before Upcott House long after midnight. Viscount Chute had joined them at the play. Seated beside Miss Postlewaite in the carriage, he yawned as they pulled up to the curb.

"Georgie, could I spend the night?" Dex suddenly asked.

Georgina smiled at her cousin. "I expected you to," she said.

Miss Postlewaite said goodnight and let the footman hand her out of the carriage. Georgina turned to Rotham. "Hugh, come in and have a cup of tea. Or whatever you want."

He hesitated. "It's awfully late."

"Come on, Hugh. You're not sleepy and neither am I."

"Aren't you ever ready to go to bed?" he asked.

"No." She shook her head as they took Dexter to the

kitchen for something to eat. "I've always considered sleep a waste of time. They've always had trouble getting me settled in at night."

"And yet there you are in the park, riding when the sun rises. I'm surprised you don't lie in bed until noon."

Georgina got a saucepan to heat some milk for Dexter's hot chocolate. She didn't like to disturb her servants this late. "Here, Dex, eat these while your milk gets hot." Georgina gave him several large teacakes and two macaroons.

"Do you want something to drink, Hugh? Some of Dexter's hot chocolate?"

"I think not. I would like a brandy, though. Stay here; I'll get it. Is it in the liquor cabinet in the library?"

"No, I took that bottle you like up to my study. I'll come with you. Dexter can take his chocolate off the stove. Can't you, Dex?"

Her cousin nodded, his mouth full of cookies, and Georgina patted his shoulder. "And you remember where you slept last week?"

"Second floor, third door to the left," mumbled Lord Chute around the edge of a large macaroon.

"That's right," Georgina laughed and led Rotham away.

In her study, Georgina turned up the lamp as Rotham walked to the side table which held the drinks. Standing in the middle of the room, she took the jeweled pins from her hair, giving a sigh of relief as she let it swirl down her back. She shook her head to loosen it. Shrugging her long ermine cloak off her shoulders, Georgina tossed it across the leather sofa.

Rotham poured brandy into a snifter. Taking his drink, he went to stand by the fire. Georgina nodded when he toasted her with his first sip.

Her eyes swept his tall figure. His evening clothes were tailored in such severe lines they would have done credit to Beau Brummel. The snowy linen of his shirt and waistcoat gleamed against the stark black of his suit; his collar points, though relatively moderate, were starched to perfection, and hours after he'd tied it, the folds of his cravat were still immaculate. He is almost too good-looking, she thought. His glinting blue-gray eyes, wide brow, and lean cheeks all contributed to his sandy blond beauty. Georgina dropped her eyes to her fingers, twining round themselves in her lap.

Rotham watched Georgina as she knelt beside the hassock, sitting sideways on the floor. The skirt of her cream-colored theatre gown was so narrow she kept her legs folded beneath her. The gleaming folds of the gossamer silk, shot through with gold threads, outlined her slender form, revealing every line. She wore a small diamond drop; this looped outside the square-cut, almost virginal neckline of her dress.

He swirled his brandy round and round, gazing into the snifter. If she's this beautiful now, he thought, what will she be when she's twenty-five?

He was leaving for Hampshire next week, taking the hot-air balloon he'd hired. More than anything in the world, Rotham wished she were going with him. They began to talk about his trip, and he thanked her for putting it in his mind.

"Yes," she said lightly. "I'm glad you're going. If only I could. To sail high and free above the clouds."

"You wouldn't be afraid, would you, Georgina?"

"No, not at all. It would be exciting beyond words. Or . . . or wouldn't it be wonderful to take your yacht this summer and sail the Aegean and study the ruins?" Georgina stopped and seemed to falter.

For a long moment he was still. Then, in a perfectly neutral tone, he said, "Yes. I've thought of that. Leave the world behind and do nothing except what one pleased for a year or even longer."

Later that night, something awakened Georgina and she thought of Rotham and his forthcoming trip to the Celtic ruins in Hampshire. Oh, but she remembered his words and hers. To sail the Aegean with Rotham and leave the world behind. They would create a world of their own. Would he take Lady Alice to the Mediterranean when she was his wife? Georgina thought he wouldn't; Lady Alice had mentioned that she wouldn't be going aboard the yacht since she was such a terrible sailor. No. Rotham would go alone. And he would never know how Georgina yearned to go with him. How could he when he had no idea of the secret locked in her heart?

Georgina closed her eyes and imagined herself rocking with the movement of the sea, the Aegean moon spilling across her bed as she reached her arms for a lover who wasn't there and never could be.

=10=

SIR PERCY MILHOUSE had a farm several miles out of town. That Saturday he invited Lady Alice, Rotham, Georgina, Lizzie, and Colly to drive there for a picnic lunch. Miss Postlewaite was visiting friends in Chelsea.

Georgina tried to stay home, but Lizzie begged her to come along. Colly wanted to go and where Colly wanted to be, there Lizzie wanted to be also.

Georgina gave in, even though she had been in a mood since the night she and Rotham had spoken of sailing the Aegean. She took herself to task and dressed in her newest walking gown for the trip to Sir Percy's farm. The dress was bright emerald green, and her soft felt hat, decorated with a long feather trailing the crown, matched it. When she saw that Rotham had elected to ride, she wished she'd brought Sultan.

Georgina had to admit it was a beautiful day, the first clear one they'd had. It was cold, but the air was brilliant with sunshine. Georgina was happy to see Lizzie enjoying herself. She talked so animatedly to Lady Alice and Colly Saltre, she didn't notice Georgina's silence. Sir Percy did.

"I hope you're not bored," he said, leaning forward to speak to Georgina, who was gazing silently out the window.

Georgina had been trying to ignore the way Rotham looked in the saddle. She turned and smiled. "No. Not at all. Isn't the sun wonderful? I was thinking of the foun-

89

tains I'm having installed this summer at Barham Hall. Have you heard about my water project?"

"Not yet," Sir Percy said gently. "Why don't you tell me all about it?"

Georgina, forcing an enthusiasm she didn't feel, began describing her problems in bringing the water from the river to the ornamental pond. "Well, Papa advised me to study the Romans, for—as he said—they moved water."

In this way, with Georgina explaining how she had amused herself during the winter months planning water elevations and circulating fountains, they passed the remainder of the trip in conversation, arriving at the farm shortly before noon.

Before this trip, Georgina hadn't seen Rotham for three days. Today, he was quieter than she'd ever known him to be. Something was wrong, she thought. All morning, whenever anyone spoke to him, his answers were short and clipped. He seemed lost in thought, remote. Georgina could feel his constraint and thought the others must, too. She glanced about. No, everyone was talking, looking through the old farm house. Lady Alice and Lizzie were supervising the unloading of the picnic baskets.

Sir Percy took Colly to see the paddocks, explaining that he intended to refurbish the farm next year and start his stud.

Rotham wandered over to an old farm wagon near the table that had been brought out for the picnic. He leaned against one wheel, smoking, his head bare in the cold air. Georgina could see the golden glints in his hair where it was struck by the sun. The sight brought treacherous tears to her eyes.

When she told Lady Alice she would walk to the top of the tall hill, Rotham dropped his cigarillo, ground it out with his boot, and said, "I'll come with you."

Georgina didn't want him. She wanted privacy, time to dry her salt tears, to get hold of her emotions.

Lady Alice and Lizzie were busily directing the placement of tablecloths and picnic plates. "Don't be long," Alice said. "We want to eat."

"Georgina," Lizzie called. "Aren't you hungry? Aren't you going to eat?"

Mistrusting her voice, Georgina mutely shook her head and scrambled up the face of the cliff in back of the house. An old path, dim and overgrown with brambles, was all she had to guide her. She could hear Rotham behind her and climbed as fast as she could.

Suddenly she reached the top and was over the crest. Rotham came up beside her, and they were alone. Georgina walked forward a few feet and stopped. They could see for miles across a large valley. Nothing moved in the land; there were no habitations. They could have been the only humans alive.

They stood on an outcropping of bare rock, ancient and chalky. At their feet a steep incline of some ten feet dropped to a narrow ledge.

Over her shoulder, Rotham said, "Stay where you are; don't go any farther!" His command was harsh, a warning to a recalcitrant child, she thought.

Georgina's tears started again, hazing her vision. She nodded, keeping her face averted. There was an ache in her throat.

She removed her hat and gloves, and as she heard him approach, her one thought was to prevent his seeing her cry. Blindly she turned aside, lifting her arm to brush at her eyes. And then she was falling.

In slow motion, or so it seemed, Georgina saw herself lurch downward as the bank gave way. The ground whirled sickeningly as she was thrown headfirst to the bottom of the incline. The only sound was the scrabble of rocks as she clutched vainly for support; then she heard Rotham's voice as he cried her name.

The gravel was sharp against Georgina's cheek. She felt the breath leave her body as the ledge broke her descent. In her wild tumble, her head struck something solid and she saw a blaze of colored lights.

Rotham saw Georgina fall. He yelled her name and followed her as fast as he could, arriving beside her in a cloud of dust and rubble.

He saw that she was already trying to get up. Georgina struggled to her knees and he assisted her to stand. Then he took his hand away.

When she moaned and held her head, Rotham felt his fright turn to anger. "I see you're all right," he said hoarsely. "Lucky little fool. I told you not to step off that cliff."

He pressed his lips together as she swayed. Blood was running down her cheek. He knew the cuts were mere scratches; he could see that. But the sight of her wounded face and hands, the evidence of recent tears, the hurt in her eyes when she raised them, all made him forget his duty.

"Georgina," he murmured, and his voice shook. The word held everything he'd been hiding these many weeks. Unable to help himself, he reached for her.

A moan of gladness came from Georgina, and her arms closed round his neck.

Rotham opened his mouth urgently, taking hers as he'd so desperately wanted to, plundering its depths, ripe, sweet, and his alone.

Small sounds, muffled urgings, came to his ears when he trailed his lips down the long lovely line of her throat.

"Oh!" Georgina cried between kisses. "Yes! That's what I've been wanting, Hugh, needing. I love . . . love you."

The earl knew he shouldn't let Georgina say such things, but her words were sweet. He ignored his conscience and kissed her more deeply.

He'd never felt like this—never wanted a woman this much before. His desire made him feel unimaginably strong and weak at the same time. He wanted—he must!—touch more of her fragrant flesh. One tiny button at Georgina's throat was all that stood in his way. This was soon undone, and he could lay his mouth against her smooth skin, feeling with his tongue the lifeblood beating there. He found her mouth open and ready when he kissed her again.

"I love you, Hugh," Georgina cried again.

Her urgently repeated words brought sanity; Rotham lifted his head. They must stop—he must stop. He pushed Georgina away from him.

Roughly he dusted her gown, setting her to rights. He snatched her hat from the ground and tried to give it to her.

But Georgina dropped it and gripped his sleeve. "Hugh?" she asked.

"No," Rotham said, answering all her unspoken queries. He forced his voice, hard and flat. "Forget this," he said. "It never happened."

Wordlessly, Georgina stared at him. Then she turned away and picked up her hat, absently smoothing the feather. She had no intention of forgetting it. The Earl of Rotham couldn't kiss her like that and not love her. And if he loved her, everything was changed.

Tomorrow she would make him admit his feelings. And tomorrow she would make him tell Lady Alice their engagement was at an end.

But Georgina didn't see the earl the next day, or the day after. Georgina waited for him to come, pacing the floor of her study; she waited until her patience was exhausted.

Tuesday night, three days after the fatal picnic, Georgina wrote him a note which brought him instantly. "Rotham," she wrote. "We must talk. If you're not in Upper Brook Street by midnight, I'm coming to Rotham House. Georgina."

It was almost eleven when the earl walked into the ballroom where Georgina was fencing with Lazy.

Rotham stood beside Tessie Granville as Georgina riposted a brilliant play by her opponent, sending his foil arcing away to land at Rotham's feet.

Something in the way the earl and Georgina were looking at one another made Lazy insist on leaving. He ruthlessly shooed the oblivious Tessie out, grabbed Dexter by the arm and insisted that they drive by the Daffy Club. He wanted to lay a bet on an upcoming prizefight, he said.

Protesting, Tessie and Dex made their adieus, and Georgina took Rotham to her study.

She splashed some brandy into a snifter, handed it to him, and said, "Why didn't you come before?"

Rotham drank and walked to the fire. "To what purpose? What is there to say?" He gazed steadily into her eyes.

But he held himself stiffly. He seemed to have retreated behind a barricade that Georgina could not breach. She saw him clench his jaw.

Never one to dodge an issue, she said, "I should think you and I need to talk about almost everything—about the fact that we love one another, about your engagement. Or don't you love me, Hugh?" She raised her chin, daring him to deny it.

He didn't bother. "Yes, I love you." He tossed off the words as if they did not contain a truth that had shaken his and Georgina's worlds to their foundations.

"And I love you," Georgina said angrily. "So what are we going to do about it?"

Rotham drained his brandy. "Nothing. We're going to do nothing."

Georgina felt the blood leave her face. "Nothing?" she asked, her tone incredulous. "You can't mean to ignore what's between us and go ahead with this nonsensical marriage to Alice de Burgh. Before, when I thought the feeling was all on my side, it was different. Now that I know you love me . . ."

"The situation has not changed, Georgina." Rotham poured himself another brandy. "I can't go to Alice and say, 'Oh, pardon me, my dear, but I made a mistake. Since I asked you to marry me, I've discovered I love Georgina Upcott. Forget our engagement, please.' Do you imagine I could do anything of the sort? That would be to lose all sense of honor, Georgina. I couldn't live with that."

"What has honor to do with this?" Georgina cried.

Rotham rounded on her. "A typically womanish reaction," he snarled. "Women never concern themselves with honor and can't understand it when men do. Don't you realize you're asking me to do what I want most in the world? And don't you know that if I give in, I'll come to hate myself and later, perhaps, hate you? Can't you see that?"

Georgina shook her head, her hair swinging wildly. "All I can see is that we love each other, and you won't do anything about it."

"And I tell you there is nothing I can do!" Rotham blazed.

"Alice de Burgh wouldn't want you if she knew you loved me," Georgina cried desperately.

Rotham laughed. "And you think that she'd want to be jilted. Think, Georgina. Could you love a man who used a woman so shabbily?"

Rotham left Georgina after that statement; he left her crying, and he walked until the dawn brought him back to Mayfair.

What he'd told Georgina was the truth: There was absolutely nothing he could do.

Later that day, he set out for Hampshire, his carriage followed by a large wagon carrying the hot-air balloon he'd hired.

=11=

IT WAS INCONCEIVABLE, Georgina thought, that the Earl of Rotham could be so obstinate, could so calmly ruin all their lives. Her anger mounted. She was glad he was gone. She hated, hated, hated Rotham!

No, she loved him, damn him. She cried for two days and hiccupped for one. Finally she got out of bed and took up her life with a vengeance, resolving to live it without restraint and to flout whatever rules that stood in her way.

Calling Gilly Driggers, Georgina put her plan into action. She would assume a masculine persona whenever she took the notion. She would dress as a young man and go with the Trio wherever they might be headed. They could take her to Tatt's to lay bets on the horses, to the clubs, to prizefights. She'd always wanted to see a prizefight. And she'd be able to drive the Silver Cloud when she wanted. She could see herself, dressed as the finest dandy, sauntering into the pit of the theater with the Trio. And Holland House. Rotham wanted her to stay away from there, did he? She would also go to Carlton House, but not very often. Old Prinny and his set were so decrepit, Georgina couldn't see herself enjoying that company. Besides, all they thought about was gambling, and Georgina didn't like to bet money. She would have to relax that rule a bit. Count her losses as the price for whatever entertainment she derived from being in various gambling hells. Oh, and she would go to Manton's and practice shooting. She'd always wanted to cup wafers in Manton's.

Georgina sent Gilly Driggers off to buy her a set of masculine small clothes and sat down to wait for the Trio to arrive. They would know which tailor could be trusted. Georgina was determined to have a coat like the one Lazy Symonds had on the last time she saw him. It looked like a Weston. She regretted it, but knew she couldn't go to a well-known tailor. Lazy would know someone who could sucessfully copy his coat. Georgina didn't aspire to look as good as Rotham, but she thought she could acquire a touch of her own.

She would show him. Only he must never know. She would never speak to him again, after their harsh parting. But she mustn't think about the earl. She would only think of her new adventure. And she mustn't forget about finding Lizzie a husband. A little over four weeks until her ball. So much to do. She needed more gowns.

Suddenly she laughed. She wondered if anyone had ever before acquired a new feminine *and* masculine wardrobe at the same time. She was still smiling when the Trio trooped into her sitting room. Without letting them know her reason, she told them of her plans to go about dressed as a man.

"But Georgina," protested Lazlo, when she divulged her scheme, "won't you have to cut your hair?"

Georgina nodded. "Yes, and I'll be glad. I'm bored with long hair."

But Georgina found that she suffered a qualm or two as her hair was being cut. The French hairdresser she had called in, a genius named M. Andre, expressed his fervent belief that the new cut he had devised for her—a type of Cherubim which could be combed into a Hero—suited her immensely, that the short natural curls tumbling over her head created the perfect foil for her beauty. Georgina had carefully explained that while she wanted a fashionable crop, she desired her long hair saved so that she might wear braids or twisted locks or a fall made of her own hair whenever she desired. Snapping his fingers in fine Gallic appreciation of this notion, Andre pronounced Mademoiselle *tres ingénieux,* yes, very clever, and promised to have the long swath ready *a toute vitesse,* at full speed.

Three nights later, Mr. George Bean, accompanied by Mr. Lazlo Symonds, Lord Chute, and Mr. T.S. Granville, strolled into the rotunda in Vauxhall Gardens.

The night was rather chilly, but George Bean didn't mind. Mr. Bean was seen to be a slender young man, dressed in the height of fashion in tan superfine. His coat excited no small comment among the crowd of Regency bucks and swells, for it fitted him to perfection, showing off his lean frame as he swaggered along with his companions. His stiff white shirt points were so high Mr. Bean had difficulty turning his head. It was necessary for him and his companions to swing themselves around to address one another. His shoulders were padded, it was true, but so discreetly that Georgina felt certain no one would know except her and her tailor. Georgina silently congratulated herself that her masquerade was going so well.

"Your cravat still ain't right," Dexter said, as they seated themselves in their box. He had spent half an hour tying it. Now he reached to straighten it.

Georgina dodged away, evading her cousin's hand. "Dexter," she exclaimed between clenched teeth. "Watch what you're doing. A man doesn't tie another man's cravat in public."

"That's right, Dex. Keep your hands off George," frowned Lazy.

"You'll ruin everything, Dex, if you're not careful," Tessie warned.

"Sorry," Dexter said. "Sorry, Georgina."

"This ain't going to work!" Tessie said.

"Yes, it is." Georgina shot a glance at Tessie and Lazy. Skewing herself around to face Dexter, she said, "Dex, you've got to remember. I am *not* Georgina. When I'm dressed like this, Georgina is somewhere else. I am Mr. George Bean. Remember how we picked my name? Say to yourself over and over that Georgina isn't here. I am

George Bean, a man, a masculine person like yourself—"

"Where is Georgina?" Dex interrupted. "What I mean is, I know this is like a play we're doing, but where would Georgina be if she wasn't here?"

"Oh, for—!" Tessie exclaimed.

Georgina shushed Tessie. Speaking in the lower register she had adopted for George Bean, she said, "Dex, I know for certain that Georgina had a dinner engagement at Lady Romsey's house tonight."

Lord Chute blinked. "She did?"

Georgina nodded. "Yes. And if you are having trouble with my name, you can call me Georgie Bean, if you find that easier. You can call me and Georgina both Georgie if you want to. Perhaps you could look on Georgie Upcott and Georgie Bean as brother and sister."

The viscount looked at her thoughtfully a full minute. "You and Georgina would have to be *natural* brother and sister," he decided. "That makes you—sorry, old boy— that makes you illegitimate, I'm afraid. Sir Owen must have had an affair and you were born sometime between Lizzie and Georgina. I mean Georgie Upcott." He ignored the stifled groans of laughter coming from Lazlo and Tessie.

Georgina looked at him admiringly. "That's wonderful, Dex, if it makes you remember that I'm Georgie Bean."

"Have it all worked out now," Dexter said happily.

The evening went swimmingly after that, and Georgina enjoyed herself immensely. The company was thin, since the weather kept many less hardy souls inside the London clubs for their entertainment. But the music was lively and the shaved ham delicious. Mr. Bean applied himself to his food and showed the world that his appetite was as good as that of his companions.

There was only one tense moment. This came at the end of their excellent dinner. Lord Rawnsley and Mr. Fenshaw Tanner lounged by. Seeing Rotham's ward and his friends, they drifted over to speak to them.

But Lazlo was up to anything. "Don't think you've met George Bean," he said. "He just got into town."

Lord Rawnsley lifted his head back and peered at Georgina. "How'd you do?" he asked politely and offered his hand.

Georgina remembered to shake hard, the way Lazy had instructed her.

"Man shouldn't shake hands like a dead fish, Georgina," Lazy said, and made her practice until her hand was sore.

Now she tightened her grip, and she and Lord Rawnsley shook heartily. Just the sort of handshake Lazlo approved. She turned to offer her hand to Mr. Tanner.

Fenshaw's handshake was everything she could have asked for too, but he kept staring at her speculatively. "Seems to me I've seen you before," he commented.

Georgina had previously seen Mr. Tanner, but only fleetingly. They'd met in the park and once in Upper Brook Street when Rotham brought his friend to call.

If she could pull this off, she thought, she could go anywhere. She opened her mouth, but Dexter spoke at that moment.

"No," Dexter said. "You're thinking of my cousin Miss Upcott. The resemblance is amazing. This is Mr. Georgie Bean. He's some sort of cousin of mine, too."

"Oh?" said Mr. Tanner blankly.

"Yes," Dexter said. "It ain't something we discuss with just everyone, but Georgie here is one of my Uncle Upcott's love children. Happens in the best of families. Known old Georgie all my life."

This bit of plain speaking gave Lord Rawnsley and Mr. Tanner something to think about. Luckily Lazy stepped in and told them that although Sir Owen acknowledged Mr. Bean, the situation wasn't generally known.

Rawnsley and Fenshaw left after shaking Mr. Bean's hand again and assuring him that they wouldn't breathe a word to a soul.

They were barely out of earshot when Tessie exploded. "If that ain't just like you, Dex," he cried. "Now you've gone and ruined everything!"

But Georgina threw up her hand. "You know, Tessie,

I don't think he has. This could start an interesting rumour and give me an unlooked for identity."

She clapped her cousin on the back. "Dexter, I think you've saved the day."

"Have I, Georgie?"

"I believe so, Dex. In fact, I couldn't have done better myself."

"Think Georgina will be pleased?" the viscount asked.

Georgina smiled and replied with great delicacy, "I think she will be just as pleased as I am."

Gilly Driggers dressed Georgina's hair for Lady Romsey's supper party and used the new fall. Georgina was delighted with the result, for it looked exactly like the style she'd worn before her haircut.

Georgina, Lizzie, and Colly arrived in Portman Square a little after nine that evening.

Lizzie was arrayed in deep blue, her bright curls threaded with silver ribbons. Georgina had on a pale golden gown which bared her arms and plunged at the neckline, showing a quite becoming décolletage. Gilly had bound Georgina in one of those new contraptions called an over the shoulder.

When the dress was in place, Gilly rolled her eyes and laughed. "Who would have thought, Miss Georgina? Last night you were a handsome young man about Town. Only think how we had to flatten your chest with that binding. And tonight? Ooh la la."

Georgina laughed, too, but she pulled at the front of her dress, working it up a little. "Do you think it's too much?"

"No," Gilly said decisively. "You want a contrast in the way you look if someone spots you as Mr. George Bean. In for a penny, in for a pound, *I* always say. When you're George Bean, look masculine. When you're yourself, Miss Georgina, look like the beautiful woman you are. And you certainly look womanly tonight. Here's your diamond drop. I put a longer chain on it so it would fall between your breasts. There. That's exactly right. Don't you think so? Come look at yourself in the long mirror."

Georgina stood before the looking glass. Her dress made her look tall and extremely slim; it was perfect, she supposed, if anyone who mattered should happen to see her in it. Putting Rotham from her mind, she tilted her head so she could see her hair. She was satisfied no one would guess she was wearing a fall.

When Georgina walked into Lady Romsey's blue salon, the first person she saw was Fenshaw Tanner. She walked straight across the room and said, "Mr. Tanner. It's been some time since I've seen you. Rotham brought you to Upcott House, I think."

Georgina swallowed a laugh as Mr. Tanner tried not to stare at her. No doubt he was comparing her to her natural brother, Mr. George Bean. Georgina wished the Trio were there so they could share the joke.

The logistics of successfully carrying out her masquerade were so involved and complicated that Georgina and the Trio found the thing challenging and exciting those first few days.

But she was the first to admit that it never could have been accomplished without the help of Gilly Driggers and Jack Haggman. Georgina left Upper Brook Street each day dressed as herself. Accompanied by Gilly and Jack, she arrived in Hampstead where she changed into Mr. George Bean.

Eventually she had masculine clothes at both places and as Mr. Bean was known to frequent Upcott House, quite often could be seen sauntering out to the front curb to take her place in the Silver Cloud. She took care never to encounter Miss Postlewaite or Lizzie when she was dressed in her masculine garb.

When she could forget Rotham, Georgina had a good time. She liked to drive the stagecoach and practiced every day, becoming quite adept at handling the ribbons.

Staying away from places where they might meet people who would know her, Georgina and the Trio went to various events and locales she'd never visited before. They drove out to Richmond Park and went to Kew Gardens. In Smithfield she saw the fair and laughed uproariously at the farce. In a gaming hell in Craven Road, she won a hundred guineas from Sir Malcom Motley. This gave her no pleasure, and she handed the money to Gilly Driggers as they drove back to Upcott House.

"Here," she said. "Didn't you say you and Jack were going to America someday? Use this to pay your passage. I can't keep it."

Georgina's one excursion into London nightlife was enough for her. "From now on," she told the Trio, "I'm only going to events in the outlying districts."

"You know, Georgina," said Lazlo, "I think that's a wise decision. Your card duel with Motley drew a lot of attention. It won't do to get George Bean too well known. Tell you what, we'll see if there's a mill in the countryside and take you to it. You'll like that."

"Will I?" she asked excitedly.

"Oh, without a doubt. Even Dex likes the prizefighters, seeing all their fine science and all. Ain't that right, Dex?"

They were at a secluded inn north of London some twelve miles. Having driven aimlessly along the country roads until their hunger overcame them, they had stopped when they came upon The Drake and Three Pigs.

The remains of their excellent dinner had been cleared away, and Dexter was seated at an old spinet in one corner of their parlor, trying to remember the waltz tune he'd heard at Maxine Ruxton's the previous evening.

"What's that song, Dexter?" Georgina asked, strolling over. She glanced into the mirror over the sideboard and ran her fingers through her hair. She rather fancied herself as a boy.

"Waltz I heard at Maxine's last night," Lord Chute murmured.

"And who is Maxine?" inquired Georgina, laying her hand on her cousin's shoulder.

"Friend of Rotham's," answered the viscount absently.

Georgina stiffened, her heart thudding in her throat. "Oh? Not a member of the ton, I take it. Where does this woman live?"

She was aware that Tessie had shot an uneasy glance at Lazy.

"In Bramerton Street," replied Dexter.

"That's in Chelsea, isn't it?" asked Georgina.

Something in the way Lazy Symonds was looking at Dexter told her that she was treading on dangerous ground. If she pursued the subject, Lazy and Tessie might warn Dexter to keep his mouth shut and she'd never find out about Rotham's convenient.

Did she really want to know? Georgina asked herself. What did she care if Rotham went to some woman in Chelsea? This more nearly concerned Lady Alice de Burgh than herself. Georgina gave a small shrug, as if settling her coat better on her shoulders. She could always get Dex alone and question him later.

She yawned as if bored with the subject. "Well, that's a very pretty waltz she taught you."

Turning to Mr. Granville, she asked, "Do you want to dance, Tessie?"

"No," Tessie said. "I can't waltz and don't want to learn."

"Let me teach you," said Georgina. "I don't want to be dancing with fortune hunters all the time. You three can help me fill my card. Come on, Tessie, I'll show you." She held out her arms.

Their waiter came to bring fresh tea and went to tell the innkeeper what he had seen. "Two of them coves is dancing with each other, capering about, whirling round and round, whilst the third is thumping that spinner fit to bust. Fourth cove is a-clapping his hands and counting one-two-three in time with the music. It's a sight such as I never thought to see."

The innkeeper sucked on his pipe awhile. Finally he was ready with his pronouncement. "Them swells is up from London, Denny. A man can't never tell what a Londoner will take it in his head to do."

=12=

AT THE SMALL inn where he was staying in Hampshire, the Earl of Rotham was having difficulty getting to sleep. Finally he swung his legs out of bed, swearing softly.

Georgina Upcott was haunting him. He had expected to miss her, but this was ridiculous. He had done everything in his power to put the girl out of his mind and concentrate on his airborne exploration of the Celtic ruins.

At any other time, he would have been entranced with flying amongst the clouds, of being wafted aloft by the bright hot-air balloon. But he found that his chief emotion was a wish to share the adventure with Georgina.

Rotham's common sense assured him that the pain he was feeling would go away in time. And not only his pain, but Georgina's, as well. This did not make his sense of loss, so acutely felt, any easier to bear. It didn't make his guilt at hurting her any less, either.

He reached for Fen Tanner's letter and forced himself to concentrate on his friend's cramped handwriting. Fen had been to Vauxhall and met a Mr. Bean and then he'd seen Georgina at Lady Romsey's party, and she looks like . . . There were some words Rotham couldn't make out that looked like *bother*. Then Fen had written several perfectly legible sentences: *Legitimate siblings frequently resemble their father's love children. Georgina certainly does, except for the long hair—which a man wouldn't have.*

Poor Fen, Rotham thought. Always in a muddle. He

tossed the letter on his bedside table and turned out the lamp. Stretching out on the bed, he watched the moonlight fill the room.

He closed his eyes and tried to imagine what Fen had meant. Georgina looked like someone named George Bean. What that had to do with love children and the length of someone's hair, he couldn't imagine.

Rotham yawned, remembering Georgina's long auburn hair the last time he'd seen her. They were at the theater with Alice and Sir Percy, and she'd worn it pulled to the top of her head and fastened with a small diamond clip. Long wispy curls fell in clusters down her bare neck. Most of the young girls were getting short crops that Season, but he distinctly remembered hearing Georgina say she wasn't going to cut hers. He'd been glad.

Rotham sighed and threw one arm over his pillow. Surely Georgina hadn't changed her mind and cut hers after all. Georgina would never . . .

Even as the words formed in his mind, the earl knew that Georgina would—and why. Swearing again, this time aloud, he reached for the lamp once more.

Rotham banged on the wall that separated his room from that of his valet's. "Belden!" he called. "Get in here!"

Belden, a thin older man who had served the earl since his Oxford days, appeared almost immediately. Although it was nearly daylight and Rotham knew he had been asleep for hours, the servant appeared wide awake and fully dressed.

"You called, my lord?" the valet asked.

"Yes," Rotham said, pulling on his riding breeches. "We're leaving for London in twenty minutes. Get the innkeeper up, pay our shot, and notify the balloon crew that our explorations are over. Here!" he tossed a large roll of notes to the servant.

"Pay them off; tell them something unexpected has come up and we are leaving."

Belden, his manner alert to his employer's every word, caught the roll when Rotham threw it. He didn't ask any questions. "Yes, my lord," was all he said.

"I know you didn't like the prizefight, Georgie," Tessie said, "but this is different. These are chickens, not men. You won't mind chickens fighting."

Georgie Bean alighted from the Silver Cloud in the early morning air. She straightened the dark beaver hat squarely on her head and stuck one hand in the pocket of her trousers. She was a complete pink of the ton today, from her nipped-in jacket to the tasseled Hessian boots on her feet; she felt quite at home in the sporting crowd gathered to watch the cockfights.

They were some fifteen miles from London, having driven out at sunrise to join the crowds congregating to see the famous Shanghai Red battle the Lancashire Cock. The gaming yard was back of a small inn called The Fighting Cock. This was on the main road, and carriages and sporting rigs were parked haphazardly all around the large barnlike structure where the cockfights took place.

Georgina went in through one of the side portals, swaggering a little, walking between Lazlo and her cousin, Dexter. They were trailed by Tessie.

"You can stay in the stagecoach if you want to, Georgie," said Lazlo. "It's right in front. This won't take long."

"No, I'm all right," Georgina said, speaking as deeply as she could. She lifted her chin. She would never admit to her qualms, being a little ashamed of her performance at the prizefight day before yesterday.

When the big fighter had landed a wisty castor, or whatever Tessie had called the hit, square on his opponent's nose, Georgina had been forced to swallow several times and avert her eyes from the blood streaming down the poor fellow's chin.

Black spots swam before Georgina's eyes, and she had slumped against Lord Chute, grasping blindly for his arm. Lazlo, after one quick look, had rustled them away, shoving Georgina into the Silver Cloud and ordering Jack Haggman to drive off immediately.

Now Lazlo glanced uneasily at Georgina. "Are you sure you feel quite the thing?"

"Never better," said Georgie Bean, looking about with interest. The cockpit was round and dug into the floor so the spectators could see every squawk and flying feather. Georgina glanced behind her. There were raised tiers of seats all around the cockpit. She was glad when Lazlo led them to seats on the bottom tier. Now she could see everything.

"These are capital seats," exclaimed Tessie. Then looking around, he said, "Georgie, see those men handling the cocks? They are the trainers. Over there," he pointed to a large well-dressed man, "is Lord Stuart. He owns the Lancashire Cock. On that side," Tessie gestured to the left, "is the man who owns the Shanghai Red, the rooster that's odds on favorite. Mr. Conyngham is a mill owner from Yorkshire."

Georgina looked at the tall heavy man wearing an old-fashioned top hat. He was dressed in riding clothes, his navy coat of superfine already wilted looking and his buff-colored breeches spattered with blood from previous fights.

Quickly, Georgina looked away. The crowd seemed to be pressing closer and closer around her. She tugged at her cravat. She must have tied it too tightly; it was choking her. And the heat! Surely it was excessive for such a clear spring morning.

Her attention was caught by the man in the center of the ring. He was calling out the names of the owners and their birds. Now the crowd hushed. The bell clanged and the handlers hurled the game cocks into the center of the pit.

In spite of everything she could do, Georgina had been unable to keep her eyes off the fighting birds.

The Lancashire Cock darted in, jumping straight up and slashing at the Red with his steel-tipped spurs. These razor-sharp gaffs attached to the rooster's natural spurs were lethal weapons. Lazy had told Georgina that one, maybe both of the birds would end the fight dead.

The Cock missed in his first assault, for the other

rooster had risen into the air at the same time for a counterslash. The red bird did not miss, and the Lancashire Cock's clipped right wing was raked and bleeding when he lit on the ground.

Both roosters fell back, the wounded bird dragging his wing. They circled for an opening, urged by their handlers and by the frenzied shouts of the crowd. There ensued an eternity while the birds darted and grappled.

"When will this be over?" shouted Georgina, clinging to Lazy Symonds's sleeve.

Lazy had started to answer when the bell rang.

The cocks were pulled apart and sponged by their trainers. These men bent over their birds, rubbing them, feeling them. Georgina saw the one holding the Shanghai Red open his mouth wide and breathe warmly over the gamecock's head, first one side and then the other. Abruptly, the bell's sharp clamor arose. Horrified, Georgina watched the poor birds thrown into the ring again. The crowd went wild, but their cries sounded distant and far away to Georgina. She raised her hand and touched her temple in a dazed manner, knocking her hat to the ground.

No, no, she thought, trying to shut her mind to the memory of all the blood. I will not swoon. But she knew she was sinking, sinking slowly, everything turning black, everything moving in slow motion.

And the last thing she saw was Rotham, looking unbelievably angry. He was reaching for her.

Georgina felt the earl lift her; he was incredibly strong. He was carrying her and Georgina tried to say his name, tried to tell Rotham how glad she was to see him. It was too late; she had passed into a vast cool darkness.

It was almost an hour and a half later that an implacable Rotham escorted Georgina into the house in Hampstead. The subdued Trio followed silently in Rotham's wake, knowing they were in for a bear-jawing and dreading it.

To Georgina the earl said, "I assume this is where you

change clothes each time. Get into your own, and after I've talked to the Trio, I'll take you to Upcott House."

This threat of talking to the Trio had the effect of rousing Georgina. She looked up and said, "Hugh, please don't be harsh with the boys. They were only doing what I asked them to." She dropped the hand she was holding out to him when she saw his face harden.

"I realize, Georgina, that they were merely doing your will, as always. What I want them to learn from this is that they can't allow feminine wiles to influence them to do what is patently foolish and wrong. I will say only what I expect Charles would have said had he come along and found they'd taken you to that cockpit."

After holding her eyes with his flinty glare a long moment, Rotham turned and left her standing in the middle of the room.

Georgina slumped down on the bed. She wouldn't cry! Damn Hugh for always being in the wrong place at the wrong time. And for being so right. That was the most humiliating aspect of the whole thing. No matter what cutting thing Rotham chose to say, she knew she deserved it.

Stepping out of the masculine garments, Georgina thought: He is holding the Trio to account for something that's my fault. Yes, this entire fiasco was my doing, my idea. The blame is mine.

Dressed in her own riding habit, she walked into the small drawing room and into the midst of a thick silence. Georgina's eyes swept the faces of her young friends. The Trio had been having a miserable time of it.

Rotham stood braced against a massive library table, his arms crossed over his chest, and Lazlo, Tessie, and Dexter sat grouped in front of him in attitudes of extreme dejection.

Rotham staightened and the Trio leapt to their feet when Georgina walked quickly into the room.

"Hugh," she began, "I—"

She was interrupted when Lazlo moved toward her and began apologizing.

"Georgina," he said, "my guardian has brought home to me, to all of us, the folly of assisting you in this mad enterprise. He has enumerated what the consequences would have been had anyone gotten wind of your male impersonation. He has also made us realize the gravity of allowing ourselves to be persuaded into some foolish endeavor by the females around us, whether they be mothers, sisters, wives, sweethearts, or childhood friends. He has pointed out that we were compromising your good name; that we should have been prepared to do what in this case is the only honorable thing. That is," Lazlo's voice broke, "to offer you marriage."

He shot an agonized glance at Rotham, swallowed audibly, and stood taller. "Georgina, I hope you can find it in your heart to forgive me, and I beg you to accept of my hand in marriage."

Tessie crowded past Lazlo, followed by Dexter. "No, mine. Georgina, you'd rather marry me than Lazy, wouldn't you?"

Dex was looking indignantly at his friends. "I'm her cousin. Georgie should marry me if she has to marry anyone. Ain't that right, Georgina?"

These proposals, more than anything, brought home the truth to Georgina. She had been in the habit of dominating the Trio while they were growing up. They trusted her judgment, and this time she had betrayed that trust.

She walked to the window and drew aside the long curtain. Looking out, pretending to entertain their proposals, Georgina let the Trio sweat a few moments. It would do them no harm and make them wary of any future situation where they would be forced to offer marriage again.

But, she wondered, what could she say? She shot a side glance at Rotham and surprised a softened, almost indulgent gleam in his eyes.

So! she thought. He appreciated the fact that she hadn't refused these marriage proposals automatically nor protested that there was no need. What can I say, she asked herself, that will let them realize what a narrow escape we've had?

Dropping the curtain, she turned and faced them. She looked at the Trio, ignoring the earl.

"Lazy," she said, "Tessie, Dexter. Dearest friends, thank you so much for your offers of marriage. As for your apologies, it is I who should apologize to you. I'm afraid that I forgot we were no longer children, free to play children's games.

"I have been thoughtless, heedless, careless beyond words. I led you into what could have ruined us all; Rotham is right about that. But luckily, no one else knows and we can trust his discretion. We seem to have gotten off more lightly than we deserve."

Georgina drew a deep breath and shook her head. "I must decline these charming offers. And I beg your forgiveness—I truly do."

Tears were streaming down Georgina's face by this time. She smiled through her tears and walked forward to offer a sisterly hug to each of the Trio in turn.

The worried looks on their faces convinced Georgina that if nothing else, her crying had brought home the gravity of the situation to them. Wordlessly the boys hugged her, and Dexter awkwardly patted her shoulder.

"We'll take you home in the Silver Cloud, Georgina," he mumbled.

Rotham spoke for the first time. "No," he said. "I'll drive her home in my curricle. Belden will ride with you."

The ride home was mostly silent. Rotham told Georgina she had handled the Trio well, but she shrugged this off.

"I couldn't very well tear down what you were building, Hugh." She tried to smile. "One of the things I most dislike in you is that you are very nearly always right. In this case, the boys had to be shown the error of their ways in trusting me, and making them propose to me has certainly taught them a lesson."

She was quiet a moment and forced herself to continue. "It has taught me a lesson as well. I was wrong, of course. I won't do it again. I've been thinking perhaps I should say I'm sick and seclude myself until my presentation."

"No," Rotham said. He had involuntarily tightened the reins, and the grays he was driving threw up their heads at this lack of control.

When he had his team in order, he said, "That's exactly what you should not do. You must make an appearance immediately. There must be no connection between George Bean's disappearance and you. You must be seen everywhere, day and night, exactly as any young fashionable would. The Trio must bring you to the park for the usual promenade at five, and then Sir Percy and I will take you and Lady Alice to the theater. We'll brush through this unscathed if we hold steady to the course."

═13═

THE TRIO, WHEN they met Georgina again, were a little reserved with her. She'd been expecting it. She knew they'd had time to realize what a tangle she'd gotten them into. And they were each contemplating the fact that if everything had been discovered, one of them would have, at this very moment, been an engaged man. It was the narrowest escape any of them had ever had. They couldn't help but hold Georgina to blame and stayed away from her for several days.

The dinner at Wolford House wasn't a success either. Lady Alice seemed to be distracted, and Sir Percy calmly declined an invitation to the opera explaining that he was attending a musical evening with Miss Gertrude Swanson, the daughter of his solicitor. "After all," he added, "she's a charming young lady."

"Making your own plans for the future?" asked Rotham.

Georgina happened to be looking directly at Lady Alice when the colonel spoke and saw that his words had an unexpected impact on their hostess.

Alice sat staring blindly at her plate, two bright spots burning high on her cheeks, and Georgina couldn't help but wonder why the thought of the colonel getting married should upset her so.

"Oh, nothing's settled," Sir Percy was saying. "I've known Miss Swanson for years. She is an admirable person, not terribly young and may suit me quite well."

Georgina thought the colonel's sidelong glance at Alice held a trace of malice. Now, why, Georgina asked herself, was Sir Percy mentioning Miss Swanson in retaliation? Was he getting even with Lady Alice because she was marrying Rotham?

Georgina looked from Alice to Sir Percy and back to Alice again. There was a pinched look about Lady Alice's mouth, and Georgina thought she was biting her lip. An interesting reaction, Georgina mused, if Lady Alice cared nothing for Sir Percy except as a good friend. Perhaps there was hope, after all.

The women left the men to their cigars, and Georgina drifted into the blue salon behind Lady Alice, Lizzie and Jane Postlewaite.

Lady Alice invited Lizzie to play the spinet and went to sit away from the light.

When the men arrived, Rotham chose to sit across the room from his betrothed, rather closer to Georgina than anyone else. He was as silent as Lady Alice, his face even harsher than it had been all through dinner.

Rotham had entered the sitting room, determined that he would say nothing at all about Georgina's gown.

She was dressed in ice blue, the tissue silk showing every line of her lissome body from the modest neckline to the plain hem.

The last thing he wanted to hear was Alice complimenting the dress, and when she asked him if he didn't agree that it was beautiful, he said, "No. I'm afraid I can't approve of silks and sophisticated colors for anyone her age. Sprig muslins seem more appropriate for young girls. Furthermore, Georgina, that hack you were riding—or attempting to ride—this afternoon in the park was dangerous."

Georgina dropped her eyes, but not before Rotham saw her blaze of anger. "I'm very proud of Rufus," she said in a steely little voice.

"You should be," Rotham said. "He's a gorgeous animal, sleek and with a magnificent head. But he's young and unschooled."

Clearly mollified at his praise of the sorrel gelding, Georgina said, "I know he's still a little headstrong and he cut up in the park today. But I handled him, didn't I? He'll be all right in a few days."

"That horse is untrustworthy, Georgina." Rotham's mouth was rigid. "I don't want you to ride him again."

His leaping heart had choked him that afternoon when he saw the horse suddenly toss his head wildly and begin to prance sideways. The beast had actually crow-hopped a time or two.

Suddenly the earl moved to the sofa and sat beside Georgina. "If you weren't an excellent horsewoman, he would have broken into a pitch in the middle of the park."

She flashed him a sparkling look of anger. "A compliment at last. At least you admit I can ride."

Abruptly Rotham changed his tactics. Ignoring the others and leaning toward her, he took her wrist in his grip.

In a low compelling tone he said, "Georgina, indulge me in this. Don't ride that horse."

Georgina's eyes opened under his intense gaze. Was this merely a case of the earl's insisting on having his way, or did he care so much for her safety? Her cheeks flamed and she looked away.

Silently she nodded, giving in, hating herself for allowing Rotham to dictate to her. But there was something about the way he was looking at her that made her want to reassure him.

He stared at her a moment longer. Then he dropped her wrist.

A warm tingle surged up Georgina's middle. She had been so miserable these last few days, thinking only of herself, of what she was feeling about his betrothal to Lady Alice. She had quite forgotten that Rotham must be suffering, too.

Georgina didn't doubt for a minute that he loved her. He had said so, and he wouldn't lie about a thing like that. She had gotten over her first unreasoning anger.

As she sipped her wine, Georgina allowed her eyes to rove the room. They came at last to Lady Alice. She could see that her hostess was still very disturbed.

Georgina wondered if the lady was upset because Rotham had been castigating her over the horse. Then she noticed the anguished glance Lady Alice sent Sir Percy Milhouse and saw their eyes lock. Georgina knew the pair was oblivious to anything going on between her and Rotham. Sir Percy was staring at Lady Alice in a way that give Georgina much to think on. Surely that was the look of a man in love.

Georgina arose long before daylight the following morning, eager to ride the new colt. She was half dressed when she remembered that Rotham had asked her not to ride Rufus again. She hadn't actually given her promise, she thought. Rotham must still be in doubt. Passing through her dark study, she decided to send him a note.

"Hugh," she wrote. "I realize that, once again, you are right. I promise not to ride Rufus until he's better schooled. Thank you for caring about my safety. Georgina."

Wishing it could have been a love letter, Georgina sealed it and wrote out Rotham's direction. She left it in her desk and headed for the stables. She would ride Sultan this morning.

She stopped short at the sight of Rotham standing beside Richard Tursdale, the head groom.

Rotham had come to make sure she didn't ride Rufus! Georgina was glad the mews were still dark. She knew her face had flushed with anger.

Only when she approached did she see that Rotham was, as her brother would have said, disguised. He stood tall and swaying. Obviously, he'd been drinking all night.

Drunk or sober, Georgina thought, Rotham should have believed in her. Furious, she grabbed him by the hand and dragged him into the house and up the stairs to her study.

The room was in shadows, lit only by the gray dawn light coming in the east windows.

Georgina found the letter and thrust it at Rotham.

"There," she said. "I was going to have that delivered to you later."

"What is it?" he asked.

Georgina shrugged. "A note telling you that I know you were right—that I promise not to ride Rufus until it's safe to do so. Or don't you believe I keep my promises?"

"The truth is, Georgina, that you didn't actually promise anything last night."

She indicated the letter again and said, "There you have it in writing."

Rotham ignored it. He was looking at her closely, his face unreadable.

He swayed, and Georgina grabbed his arm to steady him. "Hugh. Are you all right?" she asked.

"No," he said, his eyes burning into hers. "I'll never be all right again. Do you know what I've been through today—through this whole night?"

Georgina backed against the table as he laid hold of her. A violent thrill of anticipation coursed through her veins.

She caught her breath as he drew her closer, holding her by her tiny pliant waist.

"I'm sorry, Georgina. I tried to stay away. I never should have come." He tightened his hands around her waist. "But I'll be able to rest now that I have your word. I know you'd never break it."

Georgina came into his embrace. Looking up, she placed her hands on his upper arms. She could feel him trembling.

"I could break you in two," he growled and pulled her roughly against him.

He bent his head but Georgina pulled back. She didn't think Rotham had changed his mind about breaking his engagement to Lady Alice. She only thought he was a little drunk and giving in to his overwhelming desire to hold her, to kiss her again. Then she realized it was what she wanted, too, more than anything in the world. She lifted her mouth.

The kiss was both marred and intensified by the knowledge that there could be no more kisses between them.

Never again, Georgina thought, would she feel his mouth on hers. Never again would she know the sweet torture of his cruel hands, holding her, locking her in his strong embrace. Never again would she stand in his arms in the silken dawn.

At last Rotham wrenched her clinging arms from his neck, putting her from him.

"I must go," he gasped. "You're not safe with me right now, Georgina."

Replacing her riding hat, she smiled up at him. "I'm always safe with you, Hugh."

His laugh was harsh. "There speaks innocence, my girl. Never in your life have you been at greater peril than in these last few moments."

He dragged her roughly from the room down the stairs and into the courtyard. "Tursdale," he called. "Saddle the black for Miss Georgina. We're going to ride in the park."

Georgina had a lot to think about that night. She understood Rotham better now. The weight he'd put on her promise and the strength of her word showed why he couldn't break his engagement to Lady Alice. He had made Alice a promise; he had given his word.

For the first time in weeks, Georgina was almost at peace. Rotham was a man well worth loving; if she had to love him from afar, she would do so until she ceased to exist.

But if that little byplay she observed between Lady Alice and Sir Percy last night meant what she thought it did, there might be a chance for her and Rotham yet. She went to sleep smiling.

The thing to do, Georgina thought as she drove with Lizzie to Wolford House the next morning, was to spend as much time with Lady Alice and Sir Percy as she could and to find a way of encouraging them to reveal their feelings to each other.

After they worked on Lord Wolford's battle and had a light luncheon, the girls withdrew to Lady Alice's sitting room for a half-hour's respite. Georgina looked at their hostess and thought she seemed nervous and over-wrought.

"Where is Sir Percy, Lady Alice?" Georgina asked.

Alice jumped. "Percy?" she asked quickly. I . . . I believe he's at his lawyer's. We might not see him today. Are you going to help Papa with his battle this afternoon?"

"For a little while, yes," Georgina told her. "I believe Mr. Saltre and Lizzie plan to stay longer than I do. I must go into the City. Sir Graham is organizing a syndicate to buy land in America and all the parties must sign letters of incorporation. Papa is meeting me there to sign for me. I've assured him I think it's a good investment."

"Yes," answered Alice. "I believe Rotham mentioned something of that. It seems strange for a young girl to have so much say in the control of her fortune. But you seem well able to handle it."

Alice sounded as if her thoughts were a million miles away, Georgina thought. She wished she could ask what Lady Alice thought about Sir Percy's friendship with the lawyer's daughter, but didn't dare.

Georgina sighed. Patience was not her long suit, but it seemed the only course.

$==14==$

GEORGINA LEFT BERKELEY SQUARE shortly after noon, driving to Sir Graham's chambers in the city. Jack Haggman sat beside her coachman, and she took Gilly along as propriety demanded.

She thought it more than possible that she would run into Rotham and wondered if he would appreciate her conciliatory gesture.

She could have saved the effort. The Earl of Rotham was indeed going in to see Sir Graham at the same time Georgina was, but she soon learned that she had failed to win his approval.

Georgina felt her elbow gripped in a familiar steel vise, and heard the earl growl, "This won't do, Georgina. I see you still insist on rattling about the City. The next time you feel it necessary to come into this part of town, you must call me. I will drive you myself. You have no business coming here alone."

Gone was the lover of the previous morning, Georgina thought.

"I brought Jack Haggman and Gilly Driggers," she protested. "What more do you want, Hugh? Six outriders and an armed guard? I could have driven myself here in an open curricle, you know."

At his thunderous "No!" Georgina laughed tauntingly.

"Oh, yes. I'm giving serious thought to a nice sporting rig and a tiger up behind me."

This was a blatant lie; such an idea had never before occurred to Georgina.

His grip on her elbow tightened. "Georgina," he rasped between clenched teeth, "you wouldn't dare."

Flinging his hand away, Georgina mounted the stairs to Sir Graham's office.

"Oh, wouldn't I?" she spat over her shoulder. "I—or rather George Bean—saw just the team the other day at Tatt's: a beautiful pair of matched bays, high steppers, both of them."

She entered Sir Graham's office smiling, giving her mentor both her hands, kissing his cheek, shaking hands with various gentlemen.

Georgina greeted city men and lords alike, kissed her father, and thought that Rotham deserved it if she did buy herself a curricle and pair. He, after all, had put her in mind of it. She could imagine his expression if she arrived in the park in a sporting rig and driving a spanking team.

The Trio had gotten over their anger with Georgina and went with her to visit the carriage dealers in Longacre that next week.

Georgina thought they might hesitate to take her in the Silver Cloud, but they were glad to do so.

"Rotham told us to keep taking you out in our stagecoach, Georgina," Tessie assured her. "We'll be glad to drive you anyplace if you bring a chaperone."

They had met in the park, and Georgina let her horse sidle close to the barrier that marked Rotten Row from the road.

"You may not want to come with me when you hear that what I'm about to do is calculated to make Rotham mad as fire," she said and grinned.

"What?" came the chorus. "What are you going to do, Georgie?"

"Nothing that can get any of us in trouble. It's just that Rotham has grown very large in his ideas of how much he can tell me to do. Now he says he doesn't want me to have a nice little curricle and pair."

"That's ridiculous," flashed Tessie.

"No harm in a curricle, Georgina," remarked Dexter.

"No," agreed Lazlo. "You could have taken a fancy to buy a high-perch phaeton."

"I don't want a phaeton," Georgina assured them. "They are awkward and too high to mount. And you three can borrow the curricle anytime you want to. I'm sure you'd enjoy it more than a phaeton."

"Yes," they agreed.

"When do you want to go, Georgie?" asked Lord Chute.

"How about tomorrow afternoon?" suggested Georgina.

When the beautiful young lady, her three very young escorts and a demure maid appeared in Mr. Lasker's showroom, he smiled as though he had just seen an easy and advantageous sale walk through the door. Two hours later, Mr. Lasker wiped his forehead with a damp handkerchief.

As they climbed into the Silver Cloud, Georgina made certain the Trio understood what she wanted. "Keep the bays in the back of your stable out there in Hampstead," she warned. "Does Rotham come out very often?"

Assured that he did not, Georgina continued. "And tomorrow, when you take delivery of the curricle, make certain you drive up around Islington. You're not likely to encounter Rotham that way."

"But Georgie," Dexter said. "Rotham is going to see your curricle sometime, isn't he? Isn't that why you're getting it? To show him he can't dictate every little thing to you?"

Georgina knew Dexter wanted to make sure he had it all down pat. She had warned him not to spill the beans about the new curricle and pair.

"That's right, Dex," she said. "But it must be a complete surprise. I want to appear in the park with my rig unexpectedly and make Rotham turn purple."

The Trio laughed heartily.

"Serves Rotham right, Georgina. He was rather high-handed over that George Bean affair. This is a harmless trick." Tessie grinned. "I wish he *will* turn purple."

"Yes," Lazlo said. "It's like old times, Georgina. You thinking up something and the suspense building and building. And at last everything going up with a bang."

They were still chuckling when Gilly, who'd been sitting quietly next to Georgina, grasped her mistress's arm as they passed into the Strand. She was staring out the carriage window at a very pretty girl walking on the arm of a swaggering, boldly dressed young man.

"That's Mattie, Miss Georgina."

"Stop the stagecoach, Tessie," commanded Georgina. "That's Gilly's sister. I want to speak to her."

Georgina was preparing to alight when Lazy grasped her arm. "Wait a minute, Georgina," he said. "There's something about that young woman's looks I can't like. Just who is she? Where does she live?"

Georgina sat back on the squabs. "Gilly has learned it's a place called Mother Claydon's."

An expression of amazed shock registered on Tessie's face, and Dexter's mouth sagged open. Lazy's lips tightened, and he quickly stuck his head out the window. "Drive on," he shouted to the coachman.

Falling back onto the seat, Lazy looked grimly at Georgina. "What do you mean by fraternizing with a resident of the most famous night house in London, my girl?" he asked.

He sounded so much like Rotham that Georgina laughed. But the Trio was not amused. They looked at her with such forbidding frowns Georgina flushed.

"I wasn't *fraternizing* with her," Georgina protested. "I've never spoken to her in my life. Look—"

"No, you look, Georgina," Lazy snapped. "The girls who live in places like that—do you know what they do? They're prostitutes," he said, when Georgina would have answered.

Georgina tried to speak, but Lazy interrupted. "You won't talk to one if we can help it."

Tessie and Dexter both nodded.

"But the circumstances . . . ," Georgina protested.

It was Tessie who cut her off this time. "Makes no difference what the circumstances are, Georgie. You can't talk to her. How did you know of her, anyway?"

"That's just it, Tessie," Georgina said eagerly. "Gilly and I saw her in Regent's Park two weeks ago. Mattie ran away from Blandford—that's the estate where Gilly and she grew up—year before last. She went into service in Piccadilly. Then she disappeared from there two months ago. Gilly has been looking for her ever since."

Georgina looked from one of the Trio to the other. "Last week when we spied her, Gilly got out of the carriage and spoke to her. It seems this terrible woman—this Mother Claydon—is keeping Mattie prisoner in that awful place. She wants to get away, and Gilly has promised to help her. Gilly and Jack went to the park to meet her last Sunday. They had an appointment, but Mattie didn't come. I suppose that woman wouldn't let her."

Dex was shaking his head. "Girl didn't seem unhappy to me. Seemed free as a bird walking along on that fellow's arm. Laughing and all."

"The point is, Georgina, you mustn't talk to her," Lazlo said earnestly. "Girls like you can't know girls like that. We'd better speak to Rotham about this."

"No!" Georgina exclaimed. "No. I promise I will let Jack Haggman take care of everything. And I won't speak to the girl again if I see her."

The Trio looked at her solemnly. "Promise, Georgina?" they asked all at once.

Lord Chute added, "Promise on a toad's eye?"

Georgina grinned at this oath from their childhood. She crossed an X over her heart. "Promise or I'll surely die," she told them. "Now stop talking about it, you're making Gilly cry."

As soon as they arrived home, Georgina took Gilly upstairs with her. "Do you think," she asked, "that Mattie was walking with a friend? Some man who admires her and will help?"

"No," said Gilly. "From what Jack tells me, he's probably a magsman or a crimp."

"What's that?" Georgina inquired, sitting at her dressing table so Gilly could brush her hair.

"Jack told me a magsman is a point runner for a gang, Miss Georgina. He finds their marks for them, usually young men who go visiting in the East End.

"These gangs roam the streets after midnight, looking for rich men to rob. A magsman dresses well, goes into the taverns, spots someone who is drunk, and follows him as he leaves. Sometimes they have pretty girls working with them. They lure the men up the alleys where they are robbed, usually after being banged over the head with a club."

"And a crimp?" asked Georgina.

"A crimp is a spotter for the king's recruiters. They help shanghai men to serve in the navy."

"I don't think Mattie would be friends with such a man," said Georgina. "You and Jack must go back to the park next Sunday. Maybe your sister will be there. If you don't see her, you must take the carriage and watch the embankment. Perhaps she'll go walking there again. See if Jack can talk to this Mother Claydon and find out how much money she'd want to let Mattie go."

=15=

IN THOSE LAST few days before her presentation at court, everyone in Georgina's world seemed at sixes and sevens. Rotham had withdrawn behind a curtain of silence—Georgina could understand that; the Trio was off somewhere; and Lady Alice and Sir Percy were acting more strangely than ever.

And Lizzie, Georgina thought. What was wrong with Lizzie? Her sister had fallen into a silent little daze, starting when anyone spoke to her and bursting into tears at the oddest moments. When Georgina inquired if Lizzie intended wearing her blue or lavender gown to Lady Romsey's ball, it precipitated a crisis of the worst kind.

They were alone in Georgina's study, and upon hearing her sister's question, Lizzie suddenly threw her embroidery aside and covered her face with her hands. Then she began sobbing as though her heart would break.

"Lizzie," Georgina exclaimed, going quickly to embrace and hold her sister. "Whatever is the matter?"

At first Lizzie would only shake her head, but at Georgina's insistence, she raised her tear-stained face and cried, "Oh, Georgie. Did you bring us up to town to find me a husband?"

Georgina's mouth tightened and she jumped to her feet. "Who told you that? Colly?" she inquired icily. Damn Colly Saltre and his prosing ways.

"Yes!" wailed Lizzie. "Please, Georgina. I don't want to marry one of these so . . . sophisticated, dashing Town

127

y scare me to death. Every time one speaks
reeze and can't utter a sound for the life of me."
Georgina hugged her, patted her, and told her not to
be such a noddy. "I'm going to wring Colly's neck for putting these absurd notions in your head, Lizzie."

Lizzie raised her head from Georgina's shoulder. "Then
you'll give up the idea of finding me a husband?" she
asked hopefully.

Georgina jumped up once more and said brusquely, "I
certainly will not. You need a husband, Lizzie. And you
might as well get used to seeing less of Colly. Forget
Colly; he's only a cousin. You're wasting your time on
him." Georgina placed her hands on her hips and looked
down at her sister.

"Don't worry, Lizzie. Never fear that I'll do anything
to upset you. You have my solemn promise: I will never
allow you to be placed in the spotlight. You were very
silly to think I would. What I will do is quietly introduce
you to any eligible parties I come across and you can take
your pick. This notion you have of being afraid of some
of these male members of the ton is ridiculous. And I
would appreciate it if you won't try to act a perfect pea-
goose and mumble into your soup and make me want to
sink in mortification when you're around them," Georgina finished brutally. Ignoring Lizzie's fresh wails, she
stalked from the room.

In her bedroom she threw herself across her counter-
pane. Nothing seemed to be going as she'd planned it.
No matter how closely she watched, and despite the
looks that passed between them, Lady Alice and Sir Percy
seemed to have gone back to their old relationship. Alice
did seem thinner, but she stayed busier than ever and
nothing was said about the colonel's having any plans
for marriage. And Rotham! She got only grim looks from
him and distant conversation. Well, at least she would
see that Lizzie ended the Season married. That would
leave her alone.

Georgina slid off her bed and walked to the window.

That was how she'd planned to live her life, wasn't it? Alone? It was what she'd always said she would do. But that was before Hugh took her in his arms and showed her what she really wanted.

Georgina touched her lips. Had Hugh really stretched his mouth across hers, roughly demanding her total surrender? She couldn't forget his kisses in that dawn when he'd come to her study. Georgina closed her eyes and leaned her head against the cool windowpane. What wouldn't she give to have him lock the door and kiss her and never stop?

Scalding tears slid down her cheeks. Georgina hugged herself and let them flow unchecked, as she cried for all the nights she would spend alone.

The night of Lady Romsey's ball, Georgina dressed in the white gauze silk. Remembering Rotham's words about girls her age, she wore no jewels but pearls. She had a short strand clasped about her throat, and Gilly had woven several long strands through her braided chignon before pinning it on her head. The short curls about her face and neck had grown, and Gilly brushed and worked these into a feathery halo about her temples and forehead.

Her gown was a simple sheath, close fitting with short puffed sleeves. The bias-cut satin slip she wore underneath glinted through the thin translucent silk like liquid silver, revealing the long lines of Georgina's body each time she moved.

Looking at herself in the glass, Georgina's mouth quirked in a bitter little smile. Rotham, no doubt, would be highly incensed over the gown, in spite of the modest neckline. She and Madame Claudine had planned well: The gown was stunningly simple, innocently cut, but totally sensuous when it was settled on her body. Oh, yes, she thought. She was learning.

She smoothed the gown more closely across her hips and picked up the tiny beaded bag Charles had given her so long ago. Then she went below to meet the Trio.

On her way down the stairs, she thought of Rotham. He had offered to escort her, but she'd refused.

"The Trio will bring me," she told him at Lady Romsey's Tuesday salon. "And you must escort Lady Alice, after all."

Perhaps she shouldn't have said it, Georgina reflected, as she ran smoothly down to meet the Trio. Rotham had flinched as if she'd hit him.

The Trio, standing in the hall, stared dumbstruck at her as she came down. Tessie's mouth had fallen open.

They were looking at her so strangely, Georgina slowed and stopped on the bottom step. Something was wrong. What could have happened? Had Rotham been hurt?

"What is it?" she cried. "What's wrong with you?"

Tessie shut his mouth, found his tongue and blurted, "You're beautiful, Georgina."

"Is that all?" Georgina asked impatiently. They had scared her to death.

"But you look so different," Lazlo complained.

"Don't be silly. I'm the same as always. They've got me all sparked up. How would you like it if they screwed up your hair and made you wear rice powder?"

Dexter had been shaking his head all this while. "Know what, Georgie?"

"What?"

"Glad I ain't a girl."

"Well, you should be," Georgina told him. Presenting her dance card she said, "Sign this, all of you. Sign it twice so I won't have to dance with all the mushrooms who think they can make me and my money happy."

Standing in the receiving line next to Lady Romsey, and after shaking hands with over three hundred guests, Georgina saw Rotham enter with Lady Alice de Burgh and Sir Percy Milhouse.

All three wore strained expressions.

Lady Alice, when she laid her cheek against Georgina's, was shaking. "I wish you a very happy evening, my dear," she whispered. Her smile was brief and she looked around for Sir Percy, groping for his arm and leaning against him when she found it.

Sir Percy congratulated Georgina on her looks and hoped she was enjoying herself, something he obviously was not. He patted Lady Alice's hand resting in the crook of his elbow and walked away with her, leaving the Earl of Rotham to give Georgina his own best wishes.

Rotham looked at Georgina with hooded eyes; she could tell nothing of what he was thinking. His congratulations were terse. His manner was that of a polite stranger, Georgina thought. He passed on very quickly after signing Georgina's dance card twice.

Turning her head, Georgina saw that he chose not to join Lady Alice and Sir Percy. He took a glass of punch from a footman and sauntered out the French doors into the garden.

If he could get through this night, Rotham thought, he could make it through the Season. He drained his glass and placed it on the low brick wall he was leaning against. The garden was large; he'd always liked it. It wasn't formal at all. His late Uncle Romsey had employed Humphry Repton's style and imitated nature.

Sprawling ornamental shrubs were laid along meandering paths. Tall trees, several of a variety the earl didn't recognize, crowded everywhere.

His aunt was an amateur horticulturist, collecting rare trees from all over the world. The garden was a series of nooks and corners, with tall clumps of grasses native to the Sudan—or perhaps the Argentine; Rotham couldn't decide which.

Benches were spaced at intervals, and in the very back a gazebo was built, containing cushions and benches. Dim lanterns were placed along the ground and in one or two of the trees. At ten o'clock the moon was rising and only the sound of the crickets echoed through the dark garden.

Rotham sat on a rustic bench and tried to get Georgina's burning image out of his mind. He had braced himself for his first glimpse of her, but nothing could have prepared him for how she looked.

That white dress, her hair, the pearls. She must know he loved pearls. He'd like to buy her all the pearls in the world, lustrous creamy pearls. He shook his head and put a thin cigar in his mouth. He would have to go back inside in a little while.

Rotham took a deep breath and released it. A couple came into the garden and he drew back farther into the shadows. Their murmurs came to him, soft and low. As the music for the dance started, he walked back into the ballroom.

Sir Graham led Georgina into the first set, and the next three she danced with the Trio.

After that, Lazlo handed her to Rotham, and she moved into his arms at last.

"Where is Lady Alice?" Georgina inquired at once.

"Resting, talking with Colonel Milhouse in the green drawing room," the earl said indifferently.

He glanced down at Georgina, then away, but his hand tightened on hers and he drew her a little nearer. The waltz was a new one, slower than most, liltingly beautiful, the strains achingly sweet.

When the earl looked at her again, Georgina had her head bent. Her eyes were closed, her long lashes brushing her cheeks.

Rotham held her, his arm around her waist, and they moved to the music as one. He watched her face until she looked up and smiled dreamily at him.

His jaw set. "Don't do that," he said in a low growl.

Georgina's eyes flew wide. "What?" she asked.

"Don't smile at me like that," he said roughly.

"But—"

"Hush, Georgina, and dance with me."

Georgina went into supper escorted by the Trio. Lizzie came to sit with her, accompanied by Colly. She glanced shyly at her sister and reached and squeezed Georgina's hand.

Georgina returned the pressure. Let her sister be at ease this one night, she thought. Next week would be early enough to start separating her from Colly. Georgina regretted it, but it had to be done. Lizzie needed a home of her own and children and Georgina was determined to get them for her.

Across the room Georgina could see Rotham talking to Sir Percy. The two men had filled their plates at the buffet and were eating; Lady Alice sat between them. She looked pale and seemed to be barely picking at her food.

Lord Rawnsley came by with a laden plate. Fenshaw Tanner was with him.

The greetings over, Mr. Tanner turned to the Trio and said, "Haven't seen that friend of yours lately. Called himself George Bean. Where is he?"

Lazlo and Tessie both stopped chewing and looked blankly at Fenshaw. Before they could decide what to say, Dex turned to Mr. Tanner.

"Georgie Bean is gone," he said. "Left the country to seek his fortune in Australia or some place, didn't he, Georgina?"

"Van Diemen's Land," corrected Lazlo quickly.

"You've both got it wrong," stated Tessie flatly. "George Bean went to India. Said he was going into trade. Ain't that right, Georgina?" he asked.

"I believe it was Australia, Tessie." Georgina smiled at Mr. Tanner and smothered her laughter.

Poor Fen, she thought. Forever destined to worry about the elusive George Bean.

As Fen and Rawnsley moved away, she leaned toward Lizzie. "I thought Lord Rawnsley looked at you quite admiringly, Lizzie. Has he signed your dance card?"

Lizzie raised startled eyes to Georgina's. Her face paled, and Georgina could see that she had become agitated.

"No, Georgina, please don't." Lizzie swallowed. "I could never . . ."

Stifling her irritation, Georgina smiled. "Don't worry, Lizzie. We'll find someone you can like. The Season is just starting."

=16=

THE FIRST TWO sets after supper were country dances. Georgina went through the first with her cousin Dexter and the second with Gregory Mandiford.

She liked Gregory well enough; she thought he was vain and silly, but saw no harm in him.

They were breathless when their dance was over and Gregory got them some lemonade. Handing it to her, he smiled. "I say, Georgina. Why don't we step into the garden and cool off a bit?"

With hardly a thought, Georgina took Gregory's arm. It was much cooler in the garden. She sipped her lemonade and wondered where Rotham had got to. She hadn't seen him since supper. Oh, well. Georgina closed her eyes and let the breeze wash over her.

"Have you seen Lady Romsey's new gazebo?" Gregory asked, maneuvering her into the white latticed summerhouse.

Lost in her thoughts of Rotham, Georgina was barely aware that Mandiford had taken her so far back into the garden.

She glanced about the gazebo, allowing him to take her empty glass, thinking what a pleasant place this would be to read of a morning. Perhaps she should build a gazebo at Barham Hall.

Georgina gasped when Gregory Mandiford slid his arms around her and kissed the side of her throat.

Pressed against him, she tried to protest, but suddenly

his lips were on hers and it wasn't at all like Rotham's kisses. She hated this, hated Gregory Mandiford.

She stiffened and Gregory lifted his head. He laughed indulgently. "Never been kissed before?" he asked lazily. "Don't worry, sweetheart, Gregory will teach you everything you need to know." He bent his head again, but a large hand tore him roughly away and sent him reeling back.

It was Rotham, his face a furious mask in the moonlight. "Go, Mandiford. Leave while you can still walk."

Gregory Mandiford cursed under his breath. He stood tall, tall as the earl. "Only if Georgina wishes it," he said and glanced at the girl.

Georgina had backed against the inside of the gazebo. She was trembling. "Yes, Gregory. Go . . . please."

Bowing stiffly, Gregory left them, and there was only the distant sound of music from the ballroom.

"Shall we go inside?" Rotham asked coldly.

Damn him! Georgina thought. Damn him! She dabbed at her eyes with the backs of her hands as they moved toward the door. I won't cry.

Later, when Rotham came to claim his dance, Georgina did her best to appear as calm as he did.

Rotham bowed, glanced at her once, and swept her round and round in an ever widening series of circles, whirling them on the tide of music. Bound together in the waltz, their bodies flowed with the rhythm, practiced and sure. Why, thought Georgina, isn't life this simple?

When the dance was over Rotham bowed his thanks, took her to Lady Romsey, and left her.

Only a few more dances and she could go home, Georgina thought. Would the evening never end?

Exhausted when she slipped into bed, Georgina thought she might like to sleep for five days. But five hours proved enough, and she rode into the park shortly after sunrise, picking up a train of admirers that included Mr. Asbury, Mr. Melton, and Viscount Darley. They had cantered the length of the park when they encountered the Earl of Rotham.

The earl pulled up and waited for Georgina and her escort.

She didn't care what Rotham thought of her, of course, but Georgina was glad she had chosen to dress in black this morning.

Her tightly fitted jacket was buttoned to the throat, showing only a white silk jabot at the high neckline. Her skirt was split, her boots black kid, and her hat—also black—was set squarely on her head, trailing a gauzy black veil down her back.

"I say, Miss Upcott," Viscount Darley said as they rode up to Rotham. "Won't you let me show you the baby ducks on the pond? Only just hatched out."

Georgina smiled at young Darley. The viscount was twenty-three, the pride of his house, still retaining his baby fat. He had been sent up to town from the family seat in Kent to get a little Town bronze. His family was wealthy; he didn't have to marry money, but it was expected of him.

Georgina raised her brows at the earl as she pulled to a halt in front of him. Rotham looked out of sorts.

"Good morning," she called, her voice clear as the fresh air. "Isn't the park beautiful today?"

She ignored the fact that Mr. Asbury's horse, a large bay, shoved against Viscount Darley's smaller black, and the young lord was forced to fall to the rear.

"Georgina," Mr. Asbury said, "if anyone takes you to see those ducks, let it be me. I am at your command, in this or any other thing."

"Me, too," Mr. Melton said. "Anything."

Mr. Melton might be a man of few words, Georgina thought, but his gaze seemed to be quite melting this morning. She glanced at Rotham to see if he noticed.

But Rotham had himself well in control. He swept Georgina and the suitors encircling her with an expressionless glance, bowed from his saddle, and acknowledged that it was indeed a beautiful day.

Georgina's eyes narrowed on him. Steadying Sultan, she turned and smiled at the gangly Mr. Melton.

"Anything?" she asked, drawling out the word.

Mr. Melton swallowed visibly. "Anything," he promised.

"Well," Georgina said. "I'm contemplating buying a curricle and pair. Do you think you could teach me to drive?"

Amid cries of "Yes!" and "Let me teach you," Rotham threw up his chin.

But Georgina was disappointed in the earl's reaction. He merely nodded, a grim smile curling one corner of his mouth.

After a moment, Georgina touched her hat brim with her small whip and rode away.

Two days later, Georgina halted her bays in a field behind a tavern up past King's Cross. "Do you think I'm ready?" she asked Lazlo. She'd been driving her new curricle for hours.

They had chosen to stay away from the heath, because Georgina was determined to surprise the Earl of Rotham when she appeared in Hyde Park that afternoon.

"Do you really want to do this, Georgina?" asked Lazy. "Somehow I get the idea that you've lost your enthusiasm for this project."

"Yes, of course I want to do it," declared Georgina. "Don't worry about it, Lazy. Just tell me if you think I can handle this pair well enough that I won't make a fool of myself in the park."

Lazy shrugged. "You're an excellent whip, Georgie. Always were. I remember you handling a gig by the time you were eleven and you had that trap at Barham Hall. As for these bays, you needn't worry about them—they have the sweetest mouths in the world. Never seen a better team, if I do say so myself."

"Yes, Lazy," Georgina said. "I'm glad you got them. We'll return to Hampstead now. I've got to be home in time to drive in the promenade in the park. You're bringing the Silver Cloud, aren't you?"

"Yes. Do you want one of us to ride with you?"

Georgina nodded. "That might be best. I want to make Rotham mad, but if he sees me alone, no telling what he'll do."

At five o'clock, the Earl of Rotham, riding between Mr. Fenshaw Tanner and Lord Rawnsley, pulled his horse to a dead stop and stared intently at something in the road edging the park.

"That's Georgina Upcott driving a curricle," declared Fenshaw, pointing.

Rawnsley had also seen what Fen was pointing at.

"Oh, yes, Hugh," he drawled. "You were right. Georgina got her curricle. She told you about it the night of her party, didn't she?"

Shooting his friend a brief glance of thanks, Rotham rode to the rail and dismounted.

He waited while Georgina, cheeks showing points of color, pulled up with a flourish. Dexter was seated beside her.

"How do you like my rig, Hugh?" Georgina called.

A small crowd of admirers had gathered. Mr. Asbury, and Mr. Melton were there, along with Viscount Darley. Gregory Mandiford reined in his gray and sat watching, a slight smile twisting his mouth. Two coaches pulled up at that moment, the Silver Cloud and Colly's berline.

Rotham's smile looked forced and his eyes were hard and narrow. He looked the curricle over, walked all around it, and patted the team.

"Nice," he said. "One of Lasker's?"

Georgina's stomach tightened as she watched Rotham. She was half ashamed of the trick she'd pulled; she wished she were a thousand miles away.

"Yes. Lasker's," she answered, scarcely aware of what she was saying.

"I like your bays too," Rotham told her.

Georgina nodded. A movement in the crowd caught her eye, and she saw that Gregory Mandiford had come as close as the crowd would let him.

"Take me up, Georgina?" He smiled intimately at her.

"No," Rotham said. "I'm going to ride with Miss Upcott. Dexter, would you get down and take my horse?"

Dex, unaware of the currents flowing around him, cheerfully said he didn't mind.

Georgina could have stopped Rotham from getting in. And she might have if Gregory Mandiford hadn't assumed so much in that look he gave her.

"Georgina?" asked Rotham, pausing before climbing into the curricle.

At least he wasn't forcing her, Georgina thought. Ignoring Mandiford, she nodded. "Rotham." It came out flatly, but everyone knew a choice had been made.

Rotham flashed her a bright glance that made her cheeks flame even higher. Then he got in and took the reins from her numb fingers.

"Smile," he said, as they drove away. "Say something to me."

And he looked down at her, his shoulder hard against her arm, his body close, his solid thigh resting along hers.

He had rescued her again, Georgina thought, trying to think of something to talk about. She should have a flow of polite nothings tripping off her tongue. People were watching. Lady Bixley and two of the patronesses of Almack's were coming toward them.

Georgina nodded pleasantly and acknowledged their waves. Perhaps it wouldn't be so bad after all. Several women in the horsey set drove curricles when they were in town. What Georgina wasn't proud of was that she had bought the rig to spite Rotham, not because she wanted it.

"It's your own fault, Hugh," she blurted, tossing her head. "You know you goaded me into this."

He raised his brows. "Did I? Only because I said you mustn't drive into the city alone? I wonder what Charles would say."

Tears flashed in her eyes like great diamonds. "Don't," she cried, wounded. "Don't say that to me."

They had driven around the park three times, Georgina holding the ribbons the last two turns.

That was enough, Rotham judged, to show everyone that Georgina had his approval in driving the curricle. He took the reins again and drove them out the park gate, headed for Upper Brook Street.

Georgina bit her lip. She could cry when she got home, she thought.

Stealing a glance at him she asked, "You hate me, don't you, Hugh?"

She blushed. She hadn't meant to say that. It was something a child would say.

Rotham looked down at her, sitting so close beside him. She looked miserable. "No," he said softly. "I don't hate you."

He left that night for Caxton, his country seat in Surrey. Rotham knew he must put some distance between himself and Georgina. He needed a new perspective. Down at Caxton, he could relax. He could ride, hunt a little, and fish for trout. He could see to the cattle and decide which fields he wanted plowed first this spring. He couldn't wait to get away.

He was ready to go before he thought of Lady Alice. It was after nine when he rode round to Berkeley Square.

Lady Alice was ready to go out. She hadn't wanted to, but Olivia Romsey and Emily Cowper had invited her to the theater and she hadn't known how to refuse.

Rotham came in the side door, dressed in riding clothes. She jumped when Benton announced him.

"Rotham!" she said. "Where are you going?"

"To Caxton. I find I must go down to the country for a few days."

He took her hand and kissed it. He couldn't bring himself to blame Ali in any of this. It wasn't her fault that he was in love with Georgina Upcott. He must be as kind as he could, he thought.

"Caxton?" she cried. "No. Why should you go there, of all places?"

Rotham flushed. "It's my home, Alice. It's where you

140

and I will live the rest of our lives. It's where I want my children to grow up."

"But I don't want to live in the country," Lady Alice said. "I thought we'd be living in Mount Street. You never uttered a word about living in Surrey."

Rotham threw back his head. "Make up your mind to like Caxton, Alice." His voice was inflexible. "That's where we're going to live."

Wordlessly Alice stared at the earl, her eyes wide. He stared back. When she didn't say anything, he turned on his heel and walked out.

=17=

Lizzie Upcott looked at Georgina and let her eyes sink to her breakfast plate.

Georgina had just dropped a bombshell and then sat there, calmly buttering her toast, as if she hadn't shattered her sister's life.

"But what am I to tell him, Georgina? Dear Colly has been in the habit of taking me everywhere. How shall I say that I don't require his escort to Lady Brumley's party?"

Georgina shrugged. "Tell him you're going with me," she said and took a bite of coddled eggs.

"That seems quite cruel, Georgina," Lizzie protested in a shaky little voice. She seemed to be having trouble speaking.

"It's not cruel at all," Georgina said. "Colly has been monopolizing your time, Lizzie. You must meet some of the men of the ton. Well, I know you've met them, but you need to get to know them better. Give them a chance to see you without Colly sitting in your pocket all the time."

"Why don't you like Colly, Georgina?" Lizzie asked tremulously.

"It's not that I don't like him," Georgina assured her sister. "He's in the way. Lizzie, have you decided you *don't* want to be married?"

"Of course I want to get married," wailed Lizzie, breaking into tears. She threw her napkin on the table and ran from the room.

Georgina's lips tightened and she helped herself to another slice of bacon. It was a shame Lizzie was crying now, but she'd be happy later, after she had a nice home and husband and a baby or two.

Georgina shoved her plate away, unable to eat any more. Rotham had left for the country without a word.

After that confrontation in the park, he had delivered her like so much baggage to Upcott House. He left her standing on the steps as he drove her curricle away. The Trio would deliver it to her tomorrow, he said, or she could keep it at his house in Hampstead if she wanted to. But she must drive it again and soon.

Georgina had been standing on the sidewalk when he told her that; Rotham had to stay on the seat to hold the bays.

"But why?" she asked. She felt she never wanted to see the rig again. "Why should I take it out if I don't want to?"

"It mustn't seem that I disapproved of it, that I constrained you to stop. How many times, Georgina, must I warn you about wagging tongues?"

Georgina had nodded her agreement, and Rotham drove away.

She felt abandoned when he left her, and when she found that he had gone to Caxton—he left the Trio a note, but not her—Georgina found her sense of loss almost more than she could bear.

The only thing Georgina could think to do was keep busy. She had to make a life for herself; she had to do it without Rotham. Lizzie needed a husband. That would give her thoughts a firm direction.

She looked about the house and thought how vacant it seemed. No, it was her life that was vacant without Rotham.

Georgina went up to her study and sat staring out the back window. Lizzie would be getting engaged to somebody before the autumn, and Lady Alice de Burgh would marry Rotham. Georgina would have to attend the wedding and listen while everyone wished them happiness.

And her foolish schemes to attract his attention, even

if the only response she could expect was anger, must stop. They only bought them both pain.

Colly had laughed at first when Lizzie told him Georgina was trying to come between them. Six days later, he was ready to listen to whatever she had to say.

Poor Colly, thought Lizzie. Beginning with the Brumley party, Georgina had succeeded in excluding him from every outing except the drive in the park.

Colly had been forced to stand by while Georgina took Lizzie to the theater with the Trio and Mr. Asbury. He had dined with Lord Wolford while Lizzie danced with Mr. Melton at the Countess of Moultan's ball.

He had failed to wrangle an invitation to Lady Jersey's Venetian breakfast, and had sat home, as he told Lizzie, unable to summon the energy to go hear a lecture of the Astrological Society.

And at Almack's, he had watched while Lizzie whirled round the floor with Viscount Darley. Colly didn't waltz himself. "It's a dance I'm sure my late mama never would have approved," he told Lizzie and Lady Romsey.

Lizzie's heart ached; she could see that poor dear Colly was as tormented as she. Luckily, Georgina couldn't bar him from coming to Upcott House each morning, and now he was with her in the yellow salon.

"Thank goodness for your calls, Colly." Lizzie pressed her handkerchief to her lips. "They are all that have sustained me these past few days."

Colly drew a deep breath and expelled it noisily through his nose.

"I fail to understand why Georgina is putting you through this, Lizzie." He took her hand. "My dear," he said, "do you dread the thought of marriage so much?"

Lizzie looked up at this. "Oh, no, Colly. It's not that I mind the idea of marriage. Indeed, marriage is something I've always desired. I want a home of my own and children. But Georgina will keep pushing me at all these nonpareils and Corinthians. They are all so rich and worldly wise. They scare me to death."

Lizzie tried to calm herself and spoke more slowly. "Georgina will end up choosing a husband for me, and she'll make me marry him, too."

"Do you know how that makes me feel, Lizzie?"

Lizzie's heart began to pound. "No, Colly, I don't. Won't you tell me?"

"Deuced queer, Lizzie," said Colly, sinking back onto the sofa. "I haven't been looking for a wife, but just now, when I think of you married to another man . . ."

He was silent so long, Lizzie nudged him. "Yes, dear Colly. Go on."

"I'll tell you what it is, Lizzie. You'd better marry me. The thought of you being forced into a marriage you are afraid of has upset me all along. I haven't been able to think of you in some man's arms without an ache in my heart. I thought that might be pity. But now I must admit how wretched I'd feel if I had to sit and watch you being married to someone else. And dammit, Lizzie, it won't do. I won't have it."

Lizzie stared at her dear love, her hands clasped over her heart. "Oh, Colly! Is it true? Do you love me as I love you? Do you really think we can marry?"

Colly gave a rumble of laughter. "Nothing in the world can stop us, Lizzie. Not even your sister Georgina."

"Can she not?" Lizzie asked doubtfully.

"No. Be a fool if she objected too strenuously. And if there's anything Georgina is not, it's a fool."

Lizzie placed her little hand on Colly's sleeve. Oh, if only she were allowed to go to Northumberland with Colly. It had been the hope of her life to be his wife and the mother of his children. To live at Wetherfield with her dear love. Nothing, no one, must be allowed to come between her and that dream.

"Colly, dearest." Lizzie blushed.

Colly seemed to think it perfectly appropriate that she address him in such terms. He took both her hands and asked tenderly, "Yes, my love?"

Georgina was looming like an ogress in Lizzie's mind. "Don't, please don't, mention a word of this to my sister.

She won't approve this marriage between us, Colly. She wants me to marry a viscount or an earl; she is determined that I make a brilliant marriage; she told me so herself. That's why she gave me all that money, so I could attract a marquess or even a duke. And don't think we can appeal to Papa. He can never stand against Georgina."

Colly, a mere baron, was forced to agree.

He and Lizzie sat awhile, trying to think what was to be done.

The matter seemed to be bogged in a stalemate. There were so many details, such plans to be laid.

Georgina, Lizzie thought desperately, would have no trouble deciding what steps to take. Surely she and Colly could manage to get married. "We'll have to elope," she cried at last.

"You can't mean that," Colly stated. "I'd have to get a special license. I don't think . . ."

"Yes, yes!" squealed Lizzie. "Don't you see, Colly? We shall go away and be married secretly, and no one can stop us. And only think. We'll be spared all the bother of a huge wedding, which I should dislike excessively. Please, Colly?"

"Know what, Lizzie?"

"What, dearest Colly?"

"When you look at me with those blue eyes and grasp my arm with your little hands and say Please, Colly, I don't think I have the power to withstand you. I find myself wanting to lay the world at your feet. Make whatever plans you want, my sweet, and I shall carry them out. We shall slip away in a night or two and be married and journey on to Wetherfield for our honeymoon."

Lizzie smiled mistily. "We must do it right away. Is tomorrow night too soon?"

"Not if that's what you want, Lizzie. And you're right. We should hurry. But we must go to Lord Wolford's this morning. We have an appointment to finish his last battle, and I wouldn't want to disappoint him or raise your sister's suspicions by doing anything unexpected. I can get the special license this afternoon. Have to see an archbishop for that, I think. Good thing York's in town. Then I'll come back here and pick you and Miss Postlewaite up for the drive in the park. We'll be seen by everyone. At midnight we shall fly. Does Georgina have anything planned for tonight?" he asked.

"No," Lizzie breathed thankfully. "Lady Romsey has canceled her Tuesday salon. The carpenters are building bowers in the grand ballroom."

"Better and better," Colly said. "All you have to do is act in a natural way around Georgina and not let her discover what we are about. Don't," he warned, "be packing a lot of clothes. Think you can carry it off?" Colly asked.

Lizzie felt strengthened by love. "Oh, Colly," she cried. "I can do anything if it means being with you."

At Wolford House, Alice de Burgh opened her desk. It had been nearly a week since Rotham left town. And after what Papa had told her last night she hadn't slept at all. Her world had fallen to pieces. She didn't know what to do.

Lady Alice looked up as her maid came into her dressing room. "What is it, Maude?" she asked.

"Miss Upcott and Miss Georgina Upcott have called, my lady. Lord Saltre is helping his lordship in his war museum this morning. The young ladies are asking for you."

When Alice walked into her sitting room, the sisters were talking, and she heard Lizzie mention the Earl of Rotham.

"Thank you for coming," Alice said politely and burst into tears.

Lizzie, who felt she could deal with anything now that plans were in train for her to marry her own dearest Colly, stepped forward and took Lady Alice into her capable arms.

"Won't you tell me what's troubling you, dear Lady Alice?" she said gently.

It was with considerable relief that Alice, in a spate of

explanations and tears, told her friend that she had discovered she was in love with Sir Percy Milhouse after becoming engaged to the Earl of Rotham.

Alice sat with Lizzie on her small sofa and blew her nose into a lace handkerchief. "And that's not the worst of it," she wailed. "Sir Percy loves me, or he used to. At least he asked for me two years ago. But Papa turned dear Percy down on account of his lack of family. As if I cared for that. It was only last night that I learned Percy had once asked for me. But it's too late. Now he has decided he might as well marry someone, and it's killing me. To think of Percy wed to someone else. Oh, if only I'd never said I'd have Rotham."

Georgina took the situation in hand, her voice calm, betraying nothing of the exaltation she was feeling.

If Lady Alice loved Sir Percy and he loved her, then Rotham's hated engagement could be broken.

"You'll have to tell Rotham when he gets back to town," she said, when she had the whole story.

But Alice was shaking her head. "I can't do that, Georgina. This is my last chance for a husband and children. Now that Percy is looking at Miss Swanson, I must forget about him and go on with my plans to marry Rotham," she said jerkily.

Georgina started to protest, but it was Lizzie who intervened. "No, Lady Alice, you mustn't do that. Something must be done."

An entrancing frown had settled itself on Lizzie's pretty forehead. "You must tell Sir Percy you love him. He would want to know. Perhaps he only turned to Miss Swanson because he still loves you and can't have you."

"Do you think so?" Lady Alice grasped at this like a lifeline.

"Yes," said Georgina. "Besides, would it be fair to marry Rotham when you love another man?"

"Rotham knows I don't love him," Alice protested.

"He wouldn't want to stand in the way of your happiness," Georgina countered.

"That's true," Alice said. "But what shall I say?"

Georgina took Alice's hand. "It's very simple. When Rotham returns say you regret it, but must release him from his promise to marry you. That an announcement must be sent to the papers. Then you may come to Sir Percy with a free conscience." It was, Georgina thought, a plan that would gain them all their goals.

Lady Alice turned to Lizzie. "Do you think I should, Lizzie?"

"Most definitely," Lizzie said, nodding her blond curls.

Animation and color crept back into Lady Alice's face. Her black eyes sparkled. "I will. I'll tell Rotham the moment he returns. Surely it can't be long. He's been gone five—no, this is the sixth day. And when I've told him our engagement is over, I'll go to Percy. Oh, dear," her voice faltered.

"What's wrong?" asked Georgina. A flutter of alarm was beating in her throat. Nothing must interfere with Alice releasing Rotham from his promise.

"Suppose Sir Percy has already committed himself to Miss Swanson? Suppose he's asking her to marry him right this moment?" Alice's voice rose hysterically. "Suppose he doesn't love me anymore?"

"That's not likely," Georgina said, her tone a soothing balm.

"Listen to me, Lady Alice. I saw the way he was looking at you at Almack's last Wednesday night. That was the look of a man who loves someone and can't have her. Didn't you remark it, Lizzie? Haven't you noticed how Sir Percy looks at Alice? Especially when he thinks no one is looking?"

"I have," Lizzie declared.

"Then . . ." Lady Alice began.

"Yes," Georgina cut her off. "I'll probably see Sir Percy in the City today. Shall I ask him to come see you?"

Alice grasped Georgina's hand thankfully. "Yes," she cried. "If you will do this for me, Georgina, I'll be eternally grateful."

Georgina smiled. It was a brilliant smile. All her ambitions hinged on Lady Alice marrying Sir Percy Milhouse. "No thanks are necessary, Lady Alice." If Rotham were free, that was better than all the thanks in the world.

That night, Georgina looked out her window at the gathering dusk and sighed. Would Rotham want her when Lady Alice released him? Thank goodness she hadn't seriously raised any eyebrows with her starts.

Georgina shivered when she thought of her reckless George Bean escapade. No wonder Rotham accused her of being careless with her reputation. And if he disapproved of her merely going into the city alone, or driving a curricle in Hyde Park, what would he think if she did something really scandalous?

She jumped as Gilly Driggers burst into the room.

"Miss Georgina!" the maid cried. "It's poor Mattie! She's to be sold to white slavers this very night! Will you help us?"

=18=

GEORGINA LEAPED TO her feet. "We've got to get her out of there," she cried. Her glance went to the window. It was fully dark now. "What time are they moving her, Gilly?"

"I don't know. As you suggested, I waited in a closed carriage outside that place with Jack on the box. Mattie finally came out alone, walking a little dog down Montague Street. We followed her, and oh, miss. She's going to be moved! Taken to another of those terrible houses. But Jack thinks it's worse than that. He thinks that Mother Claydon has sold my sister to some bad men. He says Mattie is probably headed for a harem in Arabia or Morocco or some other heathen place."

"But you have no idea when this is taking place?" Georgina asked.

Gilly shook her head. "Mattie said tonight."

Georgina pressed her lips together. Why did Rotham have to be out of town just when she needed him so badly? The Trio, too. Someone would have to get into Mother Claydon's and rescue Mattie Driggers before she was lost forever. But who?

Briefly Georgina thought of Colly Saltre. Almost immediately she rejected the idea. He wouldn't do at all.

Whom could she trust? The Trio was at that party down in Kensington, so she couldn't reach them. Sir Percy was visiting Lady Alice; he was probably in Bruton Street right now.

Georgina swallowed. She would have to go herself,

dressed as George Bean. And if Rotham ever found out she'd gone to a flash house, he'd never ask her to marry him. If *anyone* found out, she would be *persona non grata* in the ton forever. No one would speak to her. Respectable young women weren't even supposed to know such places existed.

What should she do? Georgina agonized.

All this time she had been dressing in George Bean's clothes. She settled her hat squarely on her head and looked around, trying to think if she'd forgotten anything.

Jack Haggman would be back with the hired carriage she had ordered any moment—she couldn't very well go to Russell Square in her own coach.

Georgina stood in the middle of the floor and thought furiously. She would drive by Rotham's house. Maybe he was home.

Georgina squared her shoulders and set her hat firmly on her head. If he wasn't, she must go alone.

Rotham had come to a difficult decision while he was in the country. He would talk to Alice. There must be a better understanding between them before they married. He realized she was terribly unhappy. Why hadn't he noticed it before? Alice wouldn't live in the country, she said. But she'd have to, if she was going to be his wife. They had much to discuss. He knew it was late; he'd ridden straight in from Caxton. He stopped briefly in Mount Street, and went directly on to Berkeley Square. He wanted to talk with Lady Alice tonight if she wasn't out.

When he knocked on the door of Wolford House, Benton assured him that Lady Alice was home and in the blue drawing room. Sir Percy Milhouse was with her. Could he show the earl up?

"No thanks, Benton. Don't bother. I know the way." Rotham ran lightly up the stairs and pushed open the carved double doors to the large withdrawing room. He recoiled. There, in the middle of the room, he beheld his betrothed locked in Sir Percy's strong embrace, being kissed within an inch of her life.

At Rotham's house in Mount Street, Georgina learned the earl had returned but gone to Wolford House. She breathed a silent prayer of thanks and tried not to think of what he would say when he saw her dressed as George Bean.

Rotham stood very still, framed in the doors of the blue drawing room at Wolford House. His eyes twinkling dangerously, he sauntered across the threshold. "I take it I'm not expected," he drawled.

Sir Percy squared his chin, still clutching Rotham's betrothed in his arms.

Lady Alice could not seem to release her hold on the colonel. She clung to his arm with all her might, as though she would have fallen without its support. Her mouth, so recently kissed, had fallen open.

Sir Percy was red as a beet. "Ah . . . ," he murmured blankly.

He must have known that what the earl had just witnessed was exactly what he wanted to see. Still, it was obvious the colonel felt he and Alice were compromised.

Colonel Milhouse tightened his arm about Lady Alice's waist and stood tall. "Rotham, I can explain," he barked in his best military manner.

Rotham had to smile then. He advanced into the room, holding out his hand. "Congratulations, sir. Too bad I didn't know you cared for Lady Alice before . . . before I proposed to her."

But Alice had found her tongue. "Rotham, forgive me. But I have loved Sir Percy without knowing it. Only recently have I learned that poor Papa turned Percy down when he asked for me some time ago; I had no idea Percy wanted me. I must ask you to release me from our betrothal." She held out her hand to the earl and he took it.

Kissing it, Rotham said, "Certainly, Alice. I wish you happy, my dear. And you, sir."

Lady Alice was searching for his ring in her pocket. "Here, Rotham. I've never worn this. Give it to someone who can love you as you deserve. As I love my own dear Percy."

With only a few more words, Rotham bowed and left them. In the street, he realized he couldn't go home; he wouldn't sleep a wink. He needed to see Georgina as soon as he could. He wanted to hold her, to kiss her breathless. He wanted to tell her he was free to marry if she would have him, that she could engage in any scheme she pleased so long as she included him. Rotham took his watch out of his pocket to check the time just as a carriage drew up to the curb.

He gasped and his face hardened when Georgina, dressed as George Bean, thrust open the door and called his name.

"Hugh! Thank God I've found you!" she cried.

An electric flash went through his body at her glad cry, but when he found out what she wanted he went cold as ice.

He felt like shaking her. But as much as he disapproved, he loved her spirit. Going to a flash house, was she? Rotham suppressed the urge to smile.

It was damned serious, really. If anyone ever found out, she would be ruined.

He bit his lip, trying to decide what to do. It would be up to him to see the thing carried off without discovery.

Rotham shook his head. He really shouldn't take her. His eyes narrowed on her, and his generous mouth drew down in a severe line.

"If we go there, Georgina, you'll do exactly as I say. Hear me? I'd get this girl out of Claydon's myself if I thought she'd come with me.

"As for you, once we're inside, you'll stay away from the light. I want you in the shadows."

He paused, shaking his head again. "This isn't proper, Georgina. You're going to see things tonight no lady of quality should ever see or know. You'll be soiled. I'd better not take you after all."

But Georgina, alarmed that Rotham might back out, grabbed his arm.

"You've got to!" she cried. "You say I'll be . . . soiled. What does that matter when it comes to saving someone from a life of shame? Forget about me! Think of Mattie. Gilly says she's headed for slavery in some sultan's harem. And even I know that's much worse than being a prostitute in London. Hugh, please! I promise the minute we're out of there, I'll forget everything I've seen or heard."

His face was pained. "You won't be able to, Georgina. You will never trust the men in your life again." Never trust me, he thought.

He took his hat off and ran long shapely fingers through his hair. What could he say to make her understand? "Men have needs, Georgina. Needs a girl like you can't understand. You'll come to hate us all."

Georgina was pale, but she stood her ground. "What is that compared to saving Mattie Driggers?"

Rotham looked at her steadily and then growled, "I only hope this Mattie is worth the sacrifice. Very well," he said. "We'll get a room and I'll ask for Mattie specifically. You can disclose your name and the fact you employ her sister. That should make her trust us. And we'll make off with her somehow."

He reached into his saddle bag, took out a long pistol, and checked the priming.

"Lost your nerve yet?" he demanded, as he shoved the pistol in one of his pockets.

Georgina swallowed. "No. It has to be done."

"That's my girl," Rotham said and grinned down at her as he handed her to her hired carriage.

He was glad to see Georgina's maid sitting inside. Jack Haggman was on the box. Good. They might need some muscle before the night was through.

"To Russell Square, Jack," Rotham shouted. "And hurry!"

Mother Claydon's was a large stone house, handsome and square, three stories tall and quite respectable looking, Georgina thought.

Rotham stepped quietly to the pavement and turned to help Georgina down.

"Drive around awhile, Jack. Give us about an hour, then park across the square in Montague Street. Have you got a watch? No? Well, listen for the church bells."

His voice hushed, he spoke to the maid. "Gilly, you stay in the carriage, no matter what. If anything should happen . . ."

Rotham's voice stopped. When he spoke again it was harsh. "Nothing is going to happen. But if we're not out by daylight, Jack, go home to Upcott House and get rid of this carriage. Take it back where you rented it. If you are questioned by Sir Owen, remember you know nothing.

"And don't worry. I will take care of Miss Georgina. Stay home, go about your usual duties. And don't mention a word about this night to anyone.

"Come, Georgina," Rotham said, propelling her toward the big dimly lit house across the street. "It's now or never."

$=19=$

In Upcott House, Lizzie peered down the long staircase before descending. It was midnight and only one small lamp burned on the table in the hall. It was turned very low; the whole house was bathed in darkness and silence.

The ticking of the huge grandfather clock, sitting solidly on its pedestal, echoed in the eerie silence.

There was an unearthly, mysterious air about the hall, the everyday furniture looming in spots of shadow like strange beasts about to spring from their lairs, ready to grab and eat one alive.

Lizzie took a deep breath and started down the stairs. Suddenly the clock boomed out its midnight chimes, striking twelve times. The loud bongs reverberated through every nerve of Lizzie's body, terrifying her so she couldn't move. I will not faint, she thought, but her knees gave way and she sat suddenly on the top step, her bag and reticule thumping ahead of her down the stairs.

The monstrous chimes finally quieted. Lizzie got shakily to her feet and straightened her hat. She rushed down the stairs, recovering her carpetbag and reticule.

In the hall she sat on a straight chair, stowing her bag neatly under it. She made herself as small as she could, thankful for the darkness. Gradually her heart stopped thudding and she breathed more easily. Colly would be here any moment. Surely he would come soon. Lizzie went over the plans they'd made. He would scratch softly on the door, she would open it, and they would be safely away.

Lizzie grew quite weary in the next ten minutes. She could see the clock from where she sat, its huge round face a pale ghost in the gloom of the hall. She was prepared when the quarter-hour bell went off with a deep melodious *bong!* The clock then sat there with its internal organs whirring and clicking as they adjusted themselves and prepared to continue counting off the minutes and hours. Oh! Would Colly never come?

Georgina stared at the large bed in the room at Mother Claydon's, her imagination creating vague scenes of wanton hedonism taking place there.

She looked at Rotham, then averted her eyes. There was a tiny settee in an alcove, and Georgina went to sit on it.

He had warned her. She'd never get over this—never get it out of her mind. She felt besmirched. She knew things even married women didn't know, and the more she knew, the more questions she thought of. She shut those questions off; she didn't want to know any more; she wanted to forget everything about Mother Claydon's.

Georgina swallowed a sob and wiped at her forehead with the back of her hand. She had to face it: She was ruined. Rotham would never want her now. And even if duty prompted him to propose, she must refuse. Beyond a doubt, this was the worst night of her life.

Colly was having a terrible night, too. His carriage axle had broken and he arrived to pick up Lizzie thirty minutes late. She was in hysterics.

By the time Colly had extricated the Trio from a most convivial party at the Seymours' in Addison Road, had convinced them that he and Lizzie were eloping and that he wanted to hire their stagecoach, he realized they were all drunk.

"Capital idea, eloping!" cried Tessie. He turned to Dex for corroboration, but Dexter, leaving the others standing in the road before the Seymour mansion, had climbed into the Silver Cloud and fallen asleep.

"Coo'grashulashuns, Lizzie," Lazlo slurred and attempted to kiss her cheek. He missed and his lips grazed her left ear.

After shaking hands with the groom, he turned and tried to mount the wheel to the box, stumbling twice before he gained the axle. "Trifle boskey," he informed Lizzie owlishly. "Be all right up here on the seat." He turned cautiously and sought the high narrow ledge beside the driver.

As Colly shoved everyone into the stagecoach, Lazlo dismounted, missed the step, stumbled, and knocked Tessie Granville into the dirt at Lizzie's feet.

Tessie, finding himself sitting squarely on the ground, expostulated. "Dammit—sorry, Lizzie. Deuce take it, Lazy! Watch what you're about!"

Lazy, discovering his friend sprawled on the verge of the street, was surprised. "What are you doing down there, Tessie? Get up. Can't be s . . . sitting down at a time like this. Must go with Lizzie while she 'lopes." This brought Lazy's erratic memory back to his question.

"Wanted to ask Lizzie something. Georgina know about this?" He swayed and grasped the door to steady himself.

"No, Lazy. I sneaked out of Upcott House leaving her asleep," Lizzie explained. "She—"

Giving a great shout of laughter, Lazlo thumped Tessie, who had managed to rise from the ground, on the back. "Hear that, Tess? Georgie don't know! Hasn't a clue! Sound asleep and here we are on ad—adven'chure of our own without her. Lizzie's own," he corrected himself. "Ven'chure. It's Lizzie's 'lopement. Hers and Colly's."

Lazlo now whacked Colly on the back and shouted, "Who'd have thought it? Colly Saltre and our Lizzie 'loping?" He groped for Colly's hand and shook it heartily again. "Thank you for asking us."

Lazy reached for the wheel. Laughing so he could hardly climb, he pulled himself aloft once more.

"Take us away," he commanded, throwing wide his hand. "Pig and Two Whistles! Drake and Two Cats! Wherever! Get going! Georgina doesn't know!" he yelled into the night. "Good joke—*wunner'ful joke*—on old Georgie!"

"Oh, Lazy, do be careful," Lizzie called up to him. "Colly, do you think he'll fall?" she asked anxiously.

"Hold tight, Lazlo," advised Colly, settling himself beside his true love. They were off at last.

Georgina struggled awake. Voices. She opened her eyes and gazed about the strange bedroom. It was a moment before she remembered where she was, and when she did, in an abhorrent rush, she sat up and looked around.

Rotham had just convinced Mattie that he did not desire her services but had come at her sister's request to rescue her.

Mattie, no longer smiling, frowned and laughed her scorn. "And how did my little sister persuade you to come, my lord? I think I've misjudged her. Perhaps she's not as innocent as I'd thought."

"There's nothing between me and your sister, Mattie. I've never said two words to her. No, I came at the behest of a friend, someone who knows Gilly better than I do. And I can assure you that your sister is exactly what she seems, an honest girl who makes her living as a maid."

Mattie shrugged crossly. "More fool she. I make in one week what she makes in a year of slaving for that high and mighty lady she works for. Oh! Why can't the little fool leave me alone? Do I try to tell her how to live her life? And haven't I tried to protect her, spare her feelings about what I've chosen to do? It was only as a last resort, your lordship, that I told her that lie this afternoon. I wanted to be rid of her and that Jack. I thought if I told them Mother was shipping me out, Gilly would forget about me and leave me alone."

"Obviously, she thinks more of you than you do her."

"That's not true. I love Gilly. I protected her as much

as I could, when we lived in the attics of Blandings Castle. I persuaded old Madame, the ancient governess, to educate us. I scrubbed floors and did errands. And I saw that Gilly did her lessons; I put it into her head that she'd do well as a personal maid or dresser to some lady. Poor Gilly wasn't beautiful. She had to plan on a life of service."

"Please reconsider, Mattie." Rotham tried once more. "Gilly is waiting in a hired coach across the street. She is expecting me to rescue you. Won't you come with me?"

"I tell you I don't want rescuing!" Mattie sulked. "I told Gilly that ripper because I'm going away tonight with Lord . . . never mind who, but he is taking me to a sweet little house all my own, and giving me my own carriage. It's what I've wanted all along. And that reminds me, my lord. I must be going now. Time is money for Mattie. I've wasted enough on this fruitless mission of yours. Or do you intend to reimburse me for time spent?"

Rotham dipped his hand into his pocket and came up with a roll of notes. He peeled off two and gave them to Mattie. "Here," he said. "I wouldn't want to think I'd interfered with your revenues."

Mattie left with a smile, and Georgina came from the shadowed alcove, her face white. She slumped numbly into a chair. All to no purpose, she thought. She had come to this place for nothing. She had forfeited all her happiness, had given up her future with Rotham for no reason. Bad enough to have come for a cause, but the girl had lied to Gilly. Mattie Driggers was in no danger; she was going to a little love nest and very happy about it. What would poor little Gilly think?

"What am I going to tell Gilly?" Georgina asked Rotham.

He shook his head.

Georgina looked away. "I've ruined myself for nothing."

"Not at all," Rotham said. "You know about Alice and Sir Percy? I'm free now. We'll talk about it tomorrow."

But Georgina was on her feet. "I won't marry anyone

161

who asks me because he thinks he has to. I may be compromised, but I'm not that desperate. Get me out of here, Rotham. Just get me out and I'll go home to Barham."

She brushed away angry tears as she struggled into her jacket. One last appearance as George Bean, she thought. Get downstairs and out to the carriage. When she got home, she'd burn these clothes. She raised her chin, trying to straighten her cravat.

Then Rotham was beside her, shoving her fingers aside. His hands were rough as he tugged and pulled, creating an approximation of a waterfall. "There," he said. "Put your hat on and let's get out of this damnable place. It will be dawn in a couple of hours."

"You don't have to come with me. . . ."

"I'm coming. I'll ride beside the carriage. No more words."

The earl gave Georgina no chance to speak as he dragged her the length of the hall and down two flights of stairs. After all their worry, there was no one to witness their descent except the porter. The hall was empty.

Once they were free of the house, Rotham looked across the street. "There they are," he said, spying the closed carriage.

"Miss Georgina. At last," Gilly cried, as the vehicle rumbled across the cobblestones. Then she asked, "Where's Mattie? Couldn't you find her? Was she already taken away?"

"No, Gilly. Mattie was there. Lord Rotham talked to her, and I was able to overhear everything that was said. My dear, I don't know how to tell you this, but Mattie didn't want to come. She refused to let us help her. She said that she's not a prisoner, and she's not being moved, only going away with someone who will . . .keep her. I really think she was trying to spare your feelings."

Gilly's face crumpled, and Georgina gathered her close in a hug.

It was a long trip to Upper Brook Street. Gilly Driggers cried all the way. Just as they pulled into North Audley, she sat up and dried her face. "Miss Georgina, thank you.

You will never know how much I appreciate what you've done for me, going to that terrible place."

Georgina smiled tiredly. "Try to put it out of your mind, Gilly. You've done all you can for Mattie. You have your own life to live; you and Jack can go to America anytime you want to."

They had drawn up in front of Upcott House. Georgina raised her head and saw that lights were blazing from the roofs to the cellars. Her father had discovered her absence.

=20=

ROTHAM, REINING IN his horse, thought the same. He dismounted and helped Georgina from the carriage.

"Let me do the talking," he murmured. They mounted the steps just as Hutchins threw the doors wide open.

Georgina could see inside, and there seemed to be hundreds of people milling about in the great hall. She saw, in addition to her father and Miss Postlewaite, Lady Romsey and dozens of servants. Everyone was looking at her and the earl with wondering eyes.

Georgina grasped at Rotham's arm. Thank God he was with her.

They entered the hall, and her papa bore down on her. "Georgina!" he thundered. "Where the devil have you been and what do you know about this elopement of Lizzie's?"

He thrust a pink sheet of paper at his errant daughter. "It says here that she has run off to marry Lord Collingswood Saltre. And there's a lot of nonsense about you not approving her dear Colly as she keeps calling him. Miss Postlewaite tells me they have been thick as thieves, like a couple of lovebirds these past few weeks. Is this some meddling of yours, Georgina?" he demanded in stentorian tones.

Georgina shrank back against Rotham. "Papa! No! I know nothing about it at all. As for Lizzie wanting to marry Colly—indeed, she never said a word to me. I certainly would have had no objection."

"Should hope not," Sir Owen bellowed. "It's up to me to object to some suitor of Lizzie's. Not that I would. Not if she wanted to marry him and he was the least bit eligible."

Sir Owen threw up one hand. "Don't try to shush me, Miss Postlewaite. Georgina is always pulling tricks. Been that way since she was a little girl; can't expect her to stop now. Confess, Georgina. This is all your doing, isn't it? Is that why you're dressed that way?"

Georgina was shaking her head. "Papa, I swear. I knew nothing of this. But we've got to stop them. Lizzie would want us with her. And she must have a proper wedding."

"Sir Owen," Miss Postlewaite said, clearly and calmly, "please come into the library. Georgina, dearest, here is the letter Lizzie left for you. Why don't you go up to your room and read it?" She was trying with her eyes to indicate that Georgina should change her clothes.

"Yes," Georgina said, absently reading Lizzie's tiny flowing script. "I will. Rotham, come with me."

The earl looked at her quickly. Her voice had been devoid of the coldness he'd felt since she had rejected him at Mother Claydon's.

He followed her up the grand staircase, shaking his head at Miss Postlewaite and winking at his aunt.

When they reached her study, Georgina tossed him Lizzie's letter. "Read that," she said, "while I go to change my clothes. Luckily, my sister has told us where they've gone. It's Stoke-Manville."

Rotham, reading the letter, bit his lip to keep from grinning. Trust Lizzie Upcott to elope and leave behind notes telling where she could be found.

Georgina was still standing in the middle of the room. "I wonder how Papa learned Lizzie was missing. Where's Gilly?" she asked, just as the maid came in. "How did Papa know of Lizzie's elopement, Gilly?"

"It was Hutchins, miss. He became suspicious, when Jack and I didn't come in. By the time Sir Owen and Miss Postlewaite came home—Lady Romsey had taken them up—the house was roused and everyone knew you and

Miss Lizzie were both gone. They found her notes and the fat was in the fire."

"I see," Georgina nodded. "However it happened, we must follow Lizzie and Colly. Will you drive my curricle, Rotham? I want to catch up with Lizzie and Colly before sunrise. Surely they can't get a clergyman to marry them in the dead of night."

"Yes, I'll take you," Rotham said, smiling faintly, "and make sure we arrive by sunrise. Are we going to tell your father?"

"I think so. He and Miss Postlewaite will probably want to follow in the carriage, and Lady Romsey might want to come, too. Could you get Tursdale to put the curricle to? There's not a moment to waste."

Running down the stairs, the earl shook his head and grinned. At least Georgina was talking to him. She had turned to him as naturally as ever.

A hand reached out and grabbed him and the earl was hauled into the blue drawing room by his Aunt Romsey.

"Why are you here, Aunt?" he inquired. "So good to see you."

"Enough of this polite chatter, Rotham!" his aunt said severely. "Where have you and Georgina Upcott come from, and why is she wearing male clothing?"

The Earl of Rotham looked at his aunt consideringly. Nothing to do except create a story out of whole cloth, he thought. Might as well make it a good one.

"You know Lord Brumley, Aunt," he stated. "You also know that I've done a job or two for the foreign office, do you not? Georgina was with me tonight. There's nothing more I can say. Reputations could fall if the truth were known. I'm afraid I've already divulged too much."

"Spying for the government, eh?" Lady Romsey raised one skeptical brow.

Rotham held her eyes with a steady gaze.

"Oh, well," she said carelessly. "I'll keep any secret you ask me to, Hugh. But have you seen Lady Alice since you returned to town?"

Rotham grinned. "Yes. Also Sir Percy Milhouse. Read

the *Times* tomorrow morning, Aunt. Sir Percy informed me earlier this evening that he and Lady Alice are engaged and that they will announce it immediately. I thought you might be interested."

"I am," Lady Romsey said. "And you? Have you no personal news for me?"

The earl seemed to hesitate. "Not," he replied, "at this precise moment. But I have hopes. However, I must hurry. Georgina wants me to ask Sir Owen if he and Miss Postlewaite would like to take their carriage and follow us to Stoke-Manville. Perhaps you'd care to join us?" he suggested.

"Wouldn't miss it for the world," Lady Romsey said and volunteered her own carriage for the journey.

Sir Owen and Miss Postlewaite were in the library. Rotham stuck his head in the door and asked if he and his aunt could come in.

"Yes, yes, Rotham. What do you think we should do?"

"Georgina and I are following Lizzie and Lord Saltre to Stoke-Manville," Rotham said. "My aunt has offered her carriage. Would you and Miss Postlewaite—"

"Exactly what we've been saying." Sir Owen turned to Miss Postlewaite. "Didn't I tell you the earl would save the day?"

"Yes," said Miss Postlewaite. "Going would be best. Thank you, Rotham. Olivia, I'm so glad you're coming with us. This is just the thing. If we can't talk them out of marrying now, at least we can be with them while the ceremony is performed. I know Lizzie must be wanting us."

Sir Owen agreed. Then he shooed everyone out. "All except Rotham," he said. "I wish he will remain for a word or two."

Both men emerged five minutes later looking satisfied.

The hall was empty. "I'll get Georgina's curricle, sir," Rotham said. "You put everyone in my aunt's coach. We must be off."

Sir Owen nodded, slapping the earl on the back. "Yes, we must hurry." He looked at Rotham, a soft grin on his face. "I couldn't be more pleased, my boy. Where's Hutchins? Oh, there you are. Hutchins, put two magnums of that champagne of mine—the '94—in Lady Romsey's carriage."

Sir Owen threw a muffler about his neck, wrapping it about him twice, leaving the tasseled ends trailing over his shoulder. "Come everyone. We're off to Stoke-Manville to see Lizzie married."

"He won't marry us?" Lizzie was crying in the nave of the village church two hours later.

The sun had just risen in the east, sending streaks of gold and magenta streaming across the blue sky. But Lizzie was oblivious to this glorious display. "The vicar won't marry us without a ring, Colly? How came you to forget one?" she sobbed.

Colly had been asking himself the same question. Beginning with his broken axle, things had gone from bad to worse. The trip to Stoke-Manville had taken four hours instead of one.

Then all had seemed in hand at last. They had arrived in the false dawn. Colly had secured rooms at the Drake and Three Pigs by the simple expedient of hiring the whole inn at an exorbitant price.

But he didn't grudge the money, not if it got him married to Lizzie. Now, after they had arrived at the church, roused the cleric and presented their special license, the man refused to go through with the ceremony. And Lizzie had taken it into her head that he'd deliberately forgotten to buy a damned ring.

"But Lizzie," Colly soothed, glancing at the vicar and the Trio standing propped against the south wall. "I'll . . . I'll borrow a ring. One of you gentlemen must have a signet ring about you."

The Trio shook their heads as one man and Lizzie crumpled in a forlorn little heap in a pew. She abandoned herself to her grief and wailed again, "Oh, Colly! How can I marry a man who could forget something as important as the ring!"

Upon those words, Georgina walked into the church, followed by Rotham.

Close behind came Sir Owen, Miss Postlewaite, and Lady Olivia Romsey. They crowded into the nave with the others.

"Georgina! Papa! Miss P.! Lady Romsey!" cried Lizzie, brightening like a flower with its face to the sun. "Oh, I wanted you so!"

Her mouth drooped again and her lower lip quivered. "Georgina, Colly didn't buy me a ring!" she moaned and fell into her sister's arms. "Mr. Lumpkin won't marry us without one."

"Poor Lizzie," Georgina said and smiled over her head into Rotham's eyes. "Don't worry. Everything is fine now. Come with me. Mr. . . . er . . . Lumpkin? Is there a small room nearby where I can be private with my sister?"

Lizzie drew sharply back and said, "No, Georgina. Not if you're going to try and talk me out of marrying my dearest Colly."

Georgina laughed. "But never in the world, Lizzie. I think Colly is perfect for you, and you for him. I can't understand why I never thought of it myself. And why on earth didn't you tell me how you felt? It would have saved me oceans of trouble. Only think of what I've gone through in this campaign of mine to find you a husband." She smiled fondly at her sister.

"You mean you approve?" Lizzie gasped.

"Certainly," Georgina said. "But it isn't up to me to approve. That's Papa's job. Better ask him. As for me, I couldn't be happier for you."

"Papa?" inquired Lizzie timidly, turning to her father. "May Colly speak to you? I know it would greatly relieve his mind."

Sir Owen took his older daughter in his arms and kissed her on the forehead. "If he'll make it quick."

Colly Saltre manfully spoke the words required of him, asking very humbly for Lizzie's hand in marriage in front of them all. "And if you will give her to me, sir, I'll promise to love, honor, and cherish. . . ."

"Yes, yes," said Sir Owen. "That's all very well, Saltre, but you'd better save that for the ceremony."

Rotham had drawn Lizzie to one side and was murmuring in her ear. A great smile wiped her tears away, and she stood on tiptoe to kiss his cheek.

"Oh, Rotham!" she cried, completely shaken out of her shyness. "That's wonderful. Thank you so much. Look, Colly. The earl just happens to have a ring in his pocket. It belonged to his grandmother. He has given it to me, so we can be married. I'm ready now," she said, a beautiful blush stealing over her cheeks.

The vicar read the ceremony as Lizzie held her mother's prayer book. Colly slipped the ring on her finger and then kissed her soundly before the entire company.

=21=

AFTER THE CEREMONY Colly took everyone back to The Drake and Three Pigs. He had bespoken a sumptuous wedding breakfast, and the host assured him the feast would be ready shortly.

Colly invited the wedding party to gather round the punch bowl where Sir Owen was supervising the uncorking of his special champagne.

The Trio surrounded Georgina after the first toasts. "Surprised you, didn't we, Georgina?" Tessie teased slyly. There was a gloating air about all three of her friends.

"Knocked me square in a bucket," Georgina admitted. "Did you three plan the getaway?"

Lazy shook his head regretfully. "Colly's carriage broke down and he rousted us out of the Seymours' party. We were all six sheets in the wind."

"Oh, no! How do you feel now?" Georgina asked. She was aware that they suffered greatly after too much celebration.

"Better," said Dexter. "And after we've had several more glasses of this capital punch, we won't feel a thing."

"Hair of the dog," Tessie said, downing his wine and heading for more.

Dexter wandered off to play the piano and Lazlo went to talk to the earl.

Georgina kissed her sister and accepted the glass of champagne Lady Romsey handed her.

Lady Romsey had been watching Rotham watch Georgina. "Georgina," she said. "Rotham says you were on a spying job for the foreign office last evening. I don't know about that; it's probably one of his round tales. What I do know is that I should have expected him to offer you a ring after he got that one back from Alice."

They had drawn apart from the company and were standing beside the fireplace. Georgina looked across the room at Rotham. He was talking with Tessie and Lazlo.

The earl said something and the boys looked surprised, laughed and sought her with their eyes. Rotham said something more and they shook their heads at Georgina. Lazy raised his glass in a silent salute.

What could Rotham be telling them? Not the truth, Georgina decided. No, it must be some version of this spying tale.

Returning her attention to Lady Romsey, Georgina said, "You're right, Lady Romsey. Rotham did ask me to marry him last night. Or rather, he indicated that he was going to propose this morning. I turned him down. Have you ever suffered from an excess of pride, your ladyship?"

"Oh, yes. I turned down my dear Hait one midnight and cried for the next three days. I thought I didn't want to marry a soldier. But a woman's heart is a funny thing, my dear. It will keep on telling her the truth, no matter what her head is saying. Do you love Rotham?"

"I think I hate him," Georgina said darkly and took a sip of her champagne.

"But that's the first step." Her ladyship applauded. "Just listen to your heart, Georgina. I spent all my life following the drum. I followed my love wherever he went; now that he's gone, I can't tell you how thankful I am I wasn't afraid to do that. Nor to swallow my silly pride and admit I was wrong to turn him down."

Georgina looked at Lady Romsey thoughtfully. "Rotham and I may not be able to attend your ball tomorrow night, Lady Romsey."

Lady Romsey's brows lifted. She put her arm around Georgina and squeezed her tiny waist.

"Good!" she exclaimed, her eyes sparkling. "I'm sure

you and my nephew can find something much more interesting to do."

Georgina remained at the side of the room when Lady Romsey returned to the circle around Lizzie.

She thought about what had happened to her in the last twelve hours. She had learned so much. Georgina had come to the realization that she must allow nothing to stand in the way of her becoming Rotham's countess. Did he still want her?

She swirled the champagne in the leaded glass she held, stealing a glance at his face. She remembered that face bent over hers, the stormy blue-gray eyes, the sharp-cut lips. She hadn't forgotten how those lips felt when they ravaged hers. Now he was watching her with narrowed eyes, his face a hard mask.

Yes, she thought, she had refused him. But that had been her foolish pride. She must let him know she'd changed her mind and was ready to be asked again. The corners of Georgina's mouth lifted in a tiny, secret smile. If Rotham wouldn't ask her, she would propose to him.

Georgina found she rather liked the idea of proposing to the earl. She would take him off somewhere, walk into his arms, and make him admit he still loved her. Then she would ask him to marry her.

Her decision made, she came swiftly to Lizzie and hugged her. Her sister was radiant in her happiness. Georgina raised her champagne. "To you and Colly, dearest Lizzie. And to love."

They all drank the toast, and Georgina's eyes met Rotham's fully at last.

He nodded as if some message had passed between them. Tossing down his champagne, he handed his glass to Tessie. His eyes still holding Georgina's, Rotham made his way around the edge of the room.

Without a word, he took her wineglass and set it on the sideboard. Grasping Georgina's wrist, he pulled her along, stopping beside Tessie.

"See that we're not disturbed, will you, Tessie? I don't want anyone knocking on that door."

Everyone in the room watched breathlessly as Rotham dragged Georgina down the hall, and Tessie moved forward to block the hallway.

Inside the small private dining room, the earl locked the door. Gaze intense, he turned and advanced.

Georgina backed against the table. Her heart pounded as she watched Rotham move toward her. She couldn't take her eyes from his. He was like some great cat straight from the jungle, she thought, silently stalking her.

"Will you marry me, Hugh? I . . . I want you."

Rotham laughed. It was a deep, exultant sound. He pulled her hard against him so she could feel his need. "You will have me," he promised.

He kissed her and she sighed. "Why didn't you ask me to marry you when we were in that terrible place, Hugh? I . . . I needed that."

"Don't you understand, Georgina? I couldn't propose to you in a *night house*!"

"But I needed to know you still loved me," she protested. "That's why I said I wouldn't marry you. I was half convinced you were doing it only out of pity."

"And now you know different?" He kissed a corner of her mouth.

"Um," she nodded. Georgina freed one hand so she could trace his lips.

Rotham kissed her fingers. "I'm glad you came to find me at Wolford House last night. Glad you wanted my help. But I'm haunted by what might have happened if I hadn't returned from the country just then."

He closed his eyes and laid his cheek against her hair, hugging her to him. "I swear, Georgina. I could go mad worrying over you. Do you realize what you've put me through these last few hours? These past weeks?"

Georgina raised herself against him, clinging with her arms around his neck. "I'll make it up to you if you'll teach me how," she murmured and Rotham kissed her again.

Still holding her, he asked, "Do you want a large wedding, Georgina?"

She seemed not to have heard him, but nuzzled her face into his neck, kissing the smooth taut skin there.

Georgina loved the way he smelled. A clean masculine scent that combined tobacco, horse, and the wine he had drunk. She ran her hands up his back, under his jacket, feeling the muscles there, smooth and hard.

He gasped and pulled her head back, his fingers tangled in her hair. "Georgina, I asked you a question," he growled between clenched teeth.

"A large wedding?" she murmured, intent on getting closer. "No."

She kissed him lightly along his chin, her lips leaving a moist little trail wherever they touched him. "No, I'd rather we ran away like Lizzie did with Colly."

Rotham's hands on her arms were bruising as he held her away so he could see her face.

"We can be back in London in an hour's time," he said, his eyes glittering. "In three I can get a special license. I'm sure Lord Brumley would give me some reason for leaving England in a hurry—some excuse—something we can say we're doing for the foreign office. We can be married and aboard my yacht by early afternoon, sailing down the Thames and headed for the channel. How would you like to spend our honeymoon sailing the Aegean, Georgina?" His voice roughened on this last question.

Georgina laughed, remembering her dreams of sailing with him—hopeless only weeks ago. She came back into his arms. "I'd like that very much," she told him, offering her mouth again.

As Hugh kissed her, the doorknob rattled. There were sounds of altercation outside and Sir Owen's voice saying, "You can't keep me from seeing my own daughter, Granville. Georgina!" he shouted. "Open up!"

The earl lifted the latch, and Georgina's father walked into the room frowning.

"Don't think you're getting away with this, my girl," he exclaimed, shaking his finger at Georgina. "You never answered my questions earlier, and Rotham distracted me. What were you doing in masculine clothing last night? Not only that, but where had you been?"

Georgina blinked, trying to think of something to say. But the earl had pulled her back against him, cradling her in his arms.

He grinned at his future father-in-law. "Shall we simply say, sir, that Georgina was busy catching a husband? You may wish us happy. Georgina has just said she'll marry me. And with your permission, we plan to wed in London this afternoon and sail with the tide."

Sir Owen's face split in a grin, and he came to take Georgina in his arms. He kissed her and shook hands with Rotham.

"I'm pleased," he said, nodding his satisfaction. Then he strode out into the hall.

"Ah ha!" he cried to no one in particular. "Two marriages in one day. We'll be famous. I'll announce it at Lizzie's wedding breakfast."

"Miss Postlewaite," Sir Owen called, disappearing from view, "wait until you hear the news!"

Suddenly he stuck his head back in the door. "Told you she'd have you, Rotham, when we discussed the marriage settlements at Upcott House this morning. I said then she'd marry you, didn't I?" And he was gone.

Georgina wanted to ask what her father meant, but the earl was kissing her again.

Avon Regency Romance

Kasey Michaels

THE CHAOTIC MISS CRISPINO
76300-1/$3.99 US/$4.99 Can

THE DUBIOUS MISS DALRYMPLE
89908-6/$2.95 US/$3.50 Can

THE HAUNTED MISS HAMPSHIRE
76301-X/$3.99 US/$4.99 Can

THE WAGERED MISS WINSLOW
76302-8/$3.99 US/$4.99 Can

Loretta Chase

THE ENGLISH WITCH 70660-1/$2.95 US/$3.50 Can

ISABELLA 70597-4/$2.95 US/$3.95 Can

KNAVES' WAGER 71363-2/$3.95 US/$4.95 Can

THE SANDALWOOD PRINCESS
71455-8/$3.99 US/$4.99 Can

THE VISCOUNT VAGABOND
70836-1/$2.95 US/$3.50 Can

Jo Beverley

EMILY AND THE DARK ANGEL
71555-4/$3.99 US/$4.99 Can

THE STANFORTH SECRETS
71438-8/$3.99 US/$4.99 Can

Avon Romantic Treasures

Unforgettable, enthralling love stories, sparkling with passion and adventure from Romance's bestselling authors

ONLY IN YOUR ARMS *by Lisa Kleypas*
76150-5/$4.50 US/$5.50 Can

LADY LEGEND *by Deborah Camp*
76735-X/$4.50 US/$5.50 Can

RAINBOWS AND RAPTURE *by Rebecca Paisley*
76565-9/$4.50 US/$5.50 Can

AWAKEN MY FIRE *by Jennifer Horsman*
76701-5/$4.50 US/$5.50 Can

ONLY BY YOUR TOUCH *by Stella Cameron*
76606-X/$4.50 US/$5.50 Can

FIRE AT MIDNIGHT *by Barbara Dawson Smith*
76275-7/$4.50 US/$5.50 Can

ONLY WITH YOUR LOVE *by Lisa Kleypas*
76151-3/$4.50 US/$5.50 Can

MY WILD ROSE *by Deborah Camp*
76738-4/$4.50 US/$5.50 Can

Avon Romances—
the best in exceptional authors and unforgettable novels!

LORD OF MY HEART   Jo Beverley
76784-8/$4.50 US/$5.50 Can

BLUE MOON BAYOU   Katherine Compton
76412-1/$4.50 US/$5.50 Can

SILVER FLAME   Hannah Howell
76504-7/$4.50 US/$5.50 Can

TAMING KATE   Eugenia Riley
76475-X/$4.50 US/$5.50 Can

THE LION'S DAUGHTER   Loretta Chase
76647-7/$4.50 US/$5.50 Can

CAPTAIN OF MY HEART   Danelle Harmon
76676-0/$4.50 US/$5.50 Can

BELOVED INTRUDER   Joan Van Nuys
76476-8/$4.50 US/$5.50 Can

SURRENDER TO THE FURY   Cara Miles
76452-0/$4.50 US/$5.50 Can

Coming Soon

SCARLET KISSES   Patricia Camden
76825-9/$4.50 US/$5.50 Can

WILDSTAR   Nicole Jordan
76622-1/$4.50 US/$5.50 Can

The WONDER of WOODIWISS

continues with the publication of
her newest novel in trade paperback—

FOREVER IN YOUR EMBRACE

☐ #89818-7
$12.50 U.S. ($15.00 Canada)

THE FLAME AND THE FLOWER
☐ #00525-5
$5.99 U.S. ($6.99 Canada)

THE WOLF AND THE DOVE
☐ #00778-9
$5.99 U.S. ($6.99 Canada)

SHANNA
☐ #38588-0
$5.99 U.S. ($6.99 Canada)

ASHES IN THE WIND
☐ #76984-0
$5.99 U.S. ($6.99 Canada)

A ROSE IN WINTER
☐ #84400-1
$5.99 U.S. ($6.99 Canada)

COME LOVE A STRANGER
☐ #89936-1
$5.99 U.S. ($6.99 Canada)

SO WORTHY MY LOVE
☐ #76148-3
$5.95 U.S. ($6.95 Canada)

America Loves Lindsey!

The Timeless Romances
of #1 Bestselling Author
Johanna Lindsey

PRISONER OF MY DESIRE 75627-7/$5.99 US/$6.99 Can
Spirited Rowena Belleme *must* produce an heir, and the magnificent Warrick deChaville is the perfect choice to sire her child—though it means imprisoning the handsome knight.

ONCE A PRINCESS 75625-0/$5.95 US/$6.95 Can
From a far off land, a bold and brazen prince came to America to claim his promised bride. But the spirited vixen spurned his affections while inflaming his royal blood with passion's fire.

GENTLE ROGUE 75302-2/$5.50 US/$6.50 Can
On the high seas, the irrepressible rake Captain James Malory is bested by a high-spirited beauty whose love of freedom and adventure rivaled his own.

WARRIOR'S WOMAN 75301-4/$4.95 US/$5.95 Can

MAN OF MY DREAMS 75626-9/$5.99 US/$6.99 Can

Coming Soon

ANGEL 75628-5/$5.99 US/$6.99 Can

America Loves Lindsey!

The Timeless Romances
of #1 Bestselling Author

PRISONER OF MY DESIRE	75627-7/$5.99 US/$6.99 Can
DEFY NOT THE HEART	75299-9/$5.50 US/$6.50 Can
SILVER ANGEL	75294-8/$5.50 US/$6.50 Can
TENDER REBEL	75086-4/$5.99 US/$6.99 Can
SECRET FIRE	75087-2/$5.50 US/$6.50 Can
HEARTS AFLAME	89982-5/$5.99 US/$6.99 Can
A HEART SO WILD	75084-8/$5.50 US/$6.50 Can
WHEN LOVE AWAITS	89739-3/$5.50 US/$6.50 Can
LOVE ONLY ONCE	89953-1/$5.50 US/$6.50 Can
BRAVE THE WILD WIND	89284-7/$5.50 US/$6.50 Can
A GENTLE FEUDING	87155-6/$5.50 US/$6.50 Can
HEART OF THUNDER	85118-0/$5.50 US/$6.50 Can
SO SPEAKS THE HEART	81471-4/$5.50 US/$6.50 Can
GLORIOUS ANGEL	84947-X/$5.50 US/$6.50 Can
PARADISE WILD	77651-0/$5.50 US/$6.50 Can
FIRES OF THE WINTER	75747-8/$5.50 US/$6.50 Can
A PIRATE'S LOVE	40048-0/$5.50 US/$6.50 Can
CAPTIVE BRIDE	01697-4/$4.95 US/$5.95 Can
TENDER IS THE STORM	89693-1/$5.50 US/$6.50 Can
SAVAGE THUNDER	75300-6/$4.95 US/$5.95 Can